PAPER TIGER

MICAH REED BOOK 8

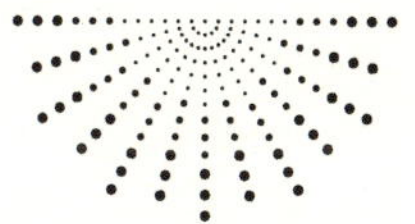

JIM HESKETT

OFFER

Want to get the Micah Reed prequel novel **Airbag Scars** for FREE? It's not available for sale **anywhere**. Check out www.jimheskett.com for this free, full-length thriller.

Also, read on after the main text for some fun, behind-the-scenes extras.

Gonna shake hands around the world
Down by the riverside
I ain't gonna study war no more
Study war no more
Ain't gonna study war no more

— TRADITIONAL

PREFACE

The events in this novel take place *before* the events in the novels AIRBAG SCARS and NAILGUN MESSIAH.

PART I

YOU CAN'T GO HOME AGAIN

PROLOGUE

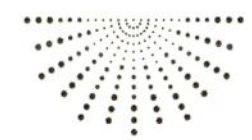

Boba Fett hasn't spoken to me all day long. I'm not sure where we stand anymore.

I clutch the sides of the sink in the bathroom until I can no longer feel my hands. Mouth so dry I can't swallow. I fear if I release, I might fly up and hit the ceiling. My heart screams in my chest, and I hardly hear anything else. *Tha-bump. Tha-bump. Tha-bump.*

My sinus passages feel clogged and my throat numb. Nothing in my body works correctly.

I stare at the inside of the sink as little droplets of blood jump from the end of my nose and plummet to the basin. *Splot. Splot. Splot.* The droplets of blood flow into pools and mix with the running water to form strings of pink and red as they circle the drain. Fractals and other patterns emerge in the streams. That one looks like a windmill. That one looks like argyle. As the designs swirl, the colors spread and change, the droplets of my vitality turning gray, and orange, then red, then black, palpitating between each different hue.

I look at myself in the mirror, and I don't recognize the face looking back; it appears to be that of a stranger. My pupils have dilated like two black marbles inside slim rings. The eyebrows look wrong; too thin. The hair is brown and always has been, but it's someone else's hair. Like a wig.

In prison, I used to stare at my hairline in the mirror and panic at the thought of it receding. I used to dig through chunks of brown to scout any gray. Now that I'm on the downslope toward thirty, I don't think about it. The descent to old age is inevitable. If this is me I'm seeing, that is.

Who is that person in the mirror?

"Micah Reed," I say. "Your name is Micah Reed. Not Michael. Micah."

Is that me? How can it be? That's not what I look like. If it's not me, then has someone else invaded the bathroom and found a way to enter the mirror and match my every movement?

You're going to die. You're going to die in this bathroom cage, and you don't even recognize your own reflection.

Those words didn't come from my lips, but they appear in my head as if someone said them. Who's inside my head? Who has wormed their way in through an open orifice?

I release my grip on the sink and stumble onto the toilet, sitting down with a thud. My limbs and torso have become exceptionally dense, and I don't know if I can rise to my feet ever again. I'm an elephant. Not literally, that would be crazy. But I am as heavy as one.

Each time my lungs expand, I can feel a thousand pounds of pressure building up in my chest cavity. It's an immense burden to operate this body.

But, am I even in control of this body?

I am trapped inside it. Without warning, my chest lurches and the alien trying to escape my stomach roars as I vomit on the floor. Some of it only makes it as far as my throat, and I gulp that back down. Like swallowing fire, I moan from the burning, acidic sensation. A quiver signals the activation of my salivary glands, and rivers of spit fill my mouth. I lean over and let the spit dribble out. *Drip drip drip.* I study the vomit on the floor and see mutating fractals again.

Hello there, fractals.

Some form of ordered chaos exists in the patterns. Did I create the fractals or do they live there already, and I discovered them after the fact?

The fractals in the vomit radiate colors, shifting from brown and green to blue and orange and back again. In the fractals, I see the answer to every question I've ever asked. Now if I just had the key. I can't translate.

I lower myself from the toilet to the floor, trying to avoid the pulsing, ever-changing mess I've made. I curl up on my side and enjoy the sensation of cold tile against my arms and head. The tile pushes against me as I push against it. Action and reaction.

The shoebox is on the floor next to me, and I remove a photograph from the top. Me and Pug in Utah, when my name was Michael McBriar. Before my arrest, before prison. Before we had any idea what was happening around us. Before moving to Denver against my will. Before Gavin Belmont and all the other insanity in my life.

A different sort of insanity then. In the picture, Pug and I are at the campsite in the desert, him smiling, dashing and handsome. Me, exhausted after hiking all morning to arrive at our destination. I didn't realize then what would happen out there in the desert, how much we would be tested over the next couple of days. How everything we thought we believed about everything would turn out to be wrong.

The person in the picture with his arm around me is dead. I can't fathom that fact. Don't want to say his name or even think it.

I want a device to wipe it from my memory. Alcohol alone hasn't worked.

I push myself to my feet and return the picture to the shoebox. Then I stash the shoebox in the cabinet above the sink, behind the bottles of cleaning liquid. The names on the bottles swirl, like they're floating in space.

I stumble out of the bathroom, into the cabin of the recreational vehicle, and each foot lands heavy as I make my way to the door. Everyone is gone, for a change. In this rare moment, the RV is quiet, a mobile house. A machine for good instead of evil.

Out into the night air of the trailer park, it's crisp. Almost cold. The trees sway in the breeze, branches like limbs slashing the air. Doing a dance with themselves, warding off the evil spirits.

Upon the hill, the house sits. I try not to think about what I saw there earlier today. The confusion and indecision I felt. But I can hear the screams in my memories. They won't go away, no matter what I do.

I'm trapped inside the screams. The screams have become me.

My stomach wants to turn again. My head feels too heavy to sit atop my body. Where is everyone else? Why is no one else out tonight in the trailer park?

Then, behind me, Ash's shotgun cocks. It's a sound I don't have to guess. It comes as easily as the resonance of a dog barking or a door slamming shut. I can see it with my mind's eye, clutched in a pair of intense hands.

I turn to see the man glowering at me. He levels the shotgun at my head. He says nothing at first, but he doesn't have to. I know he wants to kill me, and I know exactly why. It's my own curiosity and meddling that has brought us to this place.

I know tonight I will die out here in this trailer park.

THREE DAYS EARLIER

CHAPTER ONE

COLORADO - NOW

This condo has become a prison. Not literally, no. I've been in prison, and this condo is clearly an improvement on an eight by ten cell with a combo sink/toilet unit. I can come and go as I please, as long as I don't leave the city without express permission from my handler.

And that's the problem. I'm still not free. I've been in Denver for a few months, and I haven't left this city once since I've been here. It's still foreign. I don't know where anything is. I know I live across the street from the REI store and near Speer Boulevard, but I can't navigate the city without using GPS. And I don't want to walk anywhere because there are always people around. You can't ever be alone in a large city like this.

Maybe I sound like I'm whining. That's fair.

I pop the cap off another Fat Tire and guzzle a third of it in one gulp. This is my fifth or sixth, and I can't taste it anymore. Might as well be water, for all it's doing for me. Seems I don't get drunk these days, only increasingly wobbly each time I rise to use the bathroom.

My condo has hardly any furniture. Every time I intend to visit a furniture store for more, the whole process feels too overwhelming. And, in some ways, a self-fulfilling surrender. If I make this place a home, then it has to become my home.

I lift my legs and set them on the coffee table in my living room. Staring at a blank television, tuned to an empty input. Everything on television either makes me sad or angry, anyway.

I have nothing of home here. My real home. Just a condo purchased for me by the United States government. I have a case worker named Gavin who hovers above me like a vulture, makes sure I'm showing up at my job, makes sure I'm not doing stupid things like logging on to social media or calling my family.

My family thinks I'm dead. That's by design. It's a horrible design, but that decision has been made, and there's no way to undo it.

I'm twenty-eight years old, and my life is over. My last birthday occurred in a literal prison. My next birthday, coming up soon, will occur in a different kind of prison.

A new prison where my old life is fading fast.

In Stillwater, Oklahoma, hidden in the ceiling in an apartment behind the plasma center, is a shoebox. A shoebox I stashed there before the feds sent me to prison. A dangerous game I played, only hours after I narrowly escaped yet another kind of prison I'd been calling home.

Seems the last half dozen years of my life have been nothing but a series of prisons.

In that shoebox lives the only remnant of the person I used to be. I can take comfort from the fact that at least there is a record. All other evidence of Michael McBriar has been wiped from the earth, buried in redacted government documents and sealed court records. And that's for everyone's protection.

When I shift on the couch, I can feel him in my pocket, so I remove the severed head of the Boba Fett action figure and set him next to me.

"Hey, Boba," I say.

Hey, Micah.

"It's still weird to hear you say that name."

It's your name now. Your legal name.

"I know, I know. Doesn't feel right, though. It's still like a Halloween costume I can't take off."

Hmm. Interesting way to put it. Rough day?

"You could say that. I'm just sitting here, trying to get drunk, but it's not working."

Thinking about the shoebox?

"Yes."

Thinking about it.

"I know what you're trying to say. Thinking about it instead of doing something about it. But what am I supposed to do? Gavin said I'm not allowed to leave Colorado without permission, which he won't give. And it's not like I can tell him about the shoebox. Or, even tell him I want to go back to Stillwater for some other reason. No way would he sign off on that trip."

Have you considered what would happen if there's a fire at that apartment? Or if they tear the building down? It's a crappy little two-apartment building. What if they demolish it to build some six-story thing?

I sit up straight. A pulse comes at the back of my eyes. No, I have not considered this. If they pull down that building, my shoebox would be destroyed, Or, even worse, discovered.

This is a big deal. A significant development I haven't considered before.

I have to get it back.

But where will I keep it? I'm not positive, but I think it might be a crime for me to have it. Actually, it's definitely a crime. Federal evidence sits in that shoebox, such as the business card with the raised image of the wolf's head. The special piece of the puzzle from my old life.

My hand moves the beer to the table, and I pick up Boba Fett and shove him in my pocket. I start to search the room for something secluded. Something no one will suspect.

I drift back along the hallway and into my bedroom.

The trim along the floor catches my eye where the carpet meets the wall.

It could work.

I kneel next to the wall and tug on the edge of the carpet. With a few strong pulls, it separates from the floor. Underneath that, there are floorboards, sticky with the residue of pale orange glue. After jiggling two, the boards come up easily, and I'm now staring at a hollow space below.

Large enough for a shoebox.

This might work.

For this to work, I need to be careful. Need to be clever. I take my phone out of my pocket and call Frank Mueller, my boss.

"Hello?"

"Hi, Frank."

"Hey, kid. Something I can do for you?"

I hesitate for a moment. Even though I've been working for Frank at Mueller Fugitive Recovery Services for a few months, I barely know the guy. I know he doesn't drink. I know he knows I do. He's never told me I had to go to an AA meeting, but he's tossed looks at me sometimes. I know those looks. The judging-but-trying-not-to-judge look.

"Do you mind if I take a couple days off work?"

"Yeah, sure. Something wrong?"

Again, I hesitate. Frank knows my handler with the US

Marshals, Gavin. They're old friends, and Gavin even got me the job with Frank after I left prison and arrived here.

I can't tell Frank my real plan.

"No, nothing's wrong. I just need a little personal time, if that's okay."

"Sure, kid. No problem. I can tend to your projects. Just check in with me by Thursday or Friday, okay?"

He ends the call, and I stare at my phone. Feeling paranoid, and also a little guilty. I've lied to him now, for my own selfish reasons. Harmless old African-American Frank has been nothing but civil to me in the short time I've known him. He's said not an unkind word on those mornings I've stumbled into work, so hungover I can do nothing but slam coffee for the first two hours of my workday.

He seems like a solid guy, but that voice in the back of my head pesters me. What if Frank talks to Gavin?

I'm not supposed to leave town.

I could get into serious, life-altering trouble as a result of doing this.

My eyes bore into the hollowed-out space under the floorboards. I have to get the shoebox back. It's mine. The only link to my past, the only way to preserve the memory of who I used to be. My old phone is gone, along with all the pictures of that old life. The only known pictures in existence of my deceased friend are two snaps I printed out at Walgreens, a few days before he died. One of us at the Riverwalk in OKC, another of us on that harrowing camping trip in Utah.

The only memories I have of him. The only memories of the old me.

This is a terrible idea. But I'm going to do it anyway.

CHAPTER TWO

COLORADO - NOW

On I-70 headed east, I formulate my plan. I'll take this highway into Kansas. Past Hays to Salina, then I'll divert onto I-135 south. That takes me to I-35, then Oklahoma Highway 51 finally delivers me to my old college town of Stillwater. It's a nine-hour trip, so I should be there tonight.

After all this, I'll recover my shoebox. Somehow. That part of the plan is the vaguest and most difficult because I don't know what to expect when I arrive. The apartment could be unrented, or it may have a family of three or four living inside. I have to break in, access the ceiling tiles, and retrieve the shoebox.

Could be easy, or it could be literally impossible.

When I looked it up on Google Maps before I left, I saw the apartment, still behind the plasma center, around the corner from Willie's Saloon. But, I've heard Google

Maps images can be out of date. Maybe it's not there anymore. I don't even know who to call to ask if the building is actually standing. I have to hope my target is accessible and let that be good enough.

So, Phase One is to recover the shoebox.

Then, I'm back on the highway tomorrow morning, and in Denver by bedtime tomorrow night. Or, maybe I'll stay a day in Stillwater. Get cheese fries at Eskimo Joe's, maybe have a beer at Willie's. Or two, or four, or six.

Or maybe not. Maybe that's pushing it. Either way, I'll take two or three days maximum off work and arrive in Denver with my shoebox, and no one will have to know about it. Shoebox goes under the floorboards, safe and secure. Then I'm back to work for Frank at the day job and back to those unpleasant, regular check-ins with Gavin.

I'm driving the Toyota Camry the government gave me. It's a piece of junk, but I have no reason to think it will give me any problems. My dad used to drive Toyotas. He loved them and was always faithful when it came time to buy new cars. Maybe he still is, but I have no idea. Part of my government-imposed social media freeze is also a ban on checking up on my family members online. Like I'm some menacing stalker with a restraining order on me.

Going to Stillwater won't change that, but it will bring a bit of the past into my present. If I can pull it off.

This can work. Maybe. As long as I don't do anything stupid like getting pulled over by the cops. I have alcohol stashed in the trunk, but I can't indulge while I'm driving. I've made an oath to myself that I won't touch a drop until I have the shoebox in my possession.

It's a difficult promise to keep, but one that should motivate me to finish what I've started.

All of these moving parts have to work in just the right ways. I'm not sure exactly what Gavin Belmont would do to me if he caught me fleeing the state without explicit approval. Technically, I think I'm on parole, but I have no regular PO. I report directly to Gavin. He might revoke me at any time and send me to prison for a decade, or maybe even the rest of my life. I wasn't clear on that point in the terms of my deal with the government.

He's a hard man. A difficult man to reason with. That's why I've decided to forgo the step of asking his permission to leave town. Whatever lie I invent about why I need to return to Oklahoma would be shot down. He'd see right through it.

Then the shoebox slips away from me, into oblivion. And that can't happen.

As the suburbs of Denver give way to the flat grasslands of eastern Colorado, my phone rings. I slip it from my pocket and check the screen, and it reads *unavailable* on the screen. I used to never answer the phone if I didn't recognize the number. But now, there's one person in particular who always calls me from an unknown number. And if I don't answer, he'll keep calling, and calling, and calling.

I sigh as I answer the phone. "Hello, Gavin."

"Micah," he says, "good morning. How are you today?"

"I'm fine."

"It's kinda loud on your end. Are you driving?"

"Yeah, I'm running some errands for Frank." As soon as the words left my mouth, I knew it was a mistake. Something easy for Gavin to check and bust me about. But I can't take it back now.

"I see. I've been thinking, and there's something we should probably talk about, just to make sure all the cards are on the table."

"Okay."

"We're not communicating well, Micah."

"What do you mean?"

I can almost hear his clenched teeth through the phone. "I don't want to be your enemy, but you're making me into one. Our conversations never end with me feeling positive, and while that's partly my fault, you're playing a role in it, too."

"I have no idea what you're talking about."

Now, his tone grows darker. "Just don't mess with me. I've done this too many times to be worked over by a lowlife like you."

I bite my tongue, resisting the urge to lash out. It's what he wants. "I'm not trying to work you over."

"If you say so."

"What did you call me about, Gavin? Is there something I can do for you?"

"Well, I just wanted to let you know I'm flying from DC to Denver on Saturday. I'd like to stop by and have lunch with you, so I wanted to make sure you're free."

My heart constricts. Saturday is only five days from now.

"Um, yeah, I'll be free."

"Excellent. I'll see you then."

CHAPTER THREE

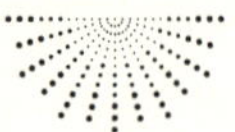

UTAH - FOUR YEARS AGO

I opened the passenger-side door of Pug's car as a line of Jeeps crawled along the dusty ground. The Wrangler at the front of the line climbed a steep sheet of Utah slick rock, crested the hill, and then descended the other side. The next Jeep in the parade soon followed, engine growling as it clawed its way up the impossibly-angled rock.

This was four years before I left Denver one morning to sneak back to Stillwater and retrieve the shoebox. Years before prison, before my relocation, before taking on a new name.

Before I knew anything.

I stretched as the stink of the Jeep engines filled my nostrils. We hadn't stopped for a break since Albuquerque, and my back was killing me. Twenty-four years old, but this thirteen-hour car ride had me feeling like an old man.

Falling asleep while sitting straight up probably hadn't helped things.

Next to the line of Jeeps, a trail map read *Elephant Hill Trailhead.* The Needles district of Canyonlands National Park. So far, we hadn't seen any needles or canyons. Mostly smaller rock formations of a pinkish-tan color. Dusty, dry, broken up by patches of little green shrubs poking out here and there through the rocks. Most of the open ground was covered with a thin layer of sand as if dropped there to act as a cushion.

I hadn't expected as much greenery in the desert as I'd seen so far. But, I supposed it had to rain from time to time. Otherwise, this would all dry up and float away with the wind.

My best friend Pug, a man my same age who I'd known since we were young, rifled through the back of his car. Pulling out various bits of camping gear, bottles, and jugs of water.

"You packed the tent poles, right, Mikey?" he said.

I stared at him across the rear of the car, my mouth dropping. Eyes full of panic. Smacked myself on the forehead. "Oh, shit."

He put his hands on his hips and scowled. "You have got to be kidding me."

I couldn't hold it any longer as a grin cracked my face.

Pug rolled his blue eyes and flicked the shaggy blond hair out of his face. "You're such a bitch."

"Yes, I am. But I dare you to tell me you don't like it. You can't do it. You just can't."

He tried to act mad, but I could see the smile at the corners of his mouth. He then checked left, right, and over his shoulder. Aside from the Jeeps, there was only one other person in the trailhead parking lot and a handful of cars. Maybe some were day hikers, some overnight backpackers.

When Pug seemed satisfied no one was looking, he reached under the front seat of his car and removed his pistol. Held it under his shirt until he could reach the back of the car. He slipped it into the side pocket of his big pack, then sighed. Gave me a tired look.

He didn't like carrying a gun any more than I did, but it was an occasional necessity of our jobs.

Pug opened the trunk and yanked out bags of clothes, the tent, sleeping bags, plus cookware. I hadn't been backpacking since high school and had brought none of my own gear when making the move to Stillwater for college. I had nothing at my part-time residence at the Freedom House in Oklahoma City, either, so we were using all Pug's gear. And he had plenty.

He hefted a second massive backpack out of the trunk and dropped it at my feet. The thing looked like an octopus, with all those attachments and nylon tendrils sticking out everywhere.

"Does the park service provide Sherpas," I asked, "or are we totally on our own?"

Pug shook his head. "That's part of the platinum package, and our budget is only for gold."

"Figures."

"You know how to put that on?" he said.

"Sure. The strappy parts go over my shoulders. Easy enough. I don't need a manual or anything."

He sighed and lifted the pack, then made me turn around. He slid it over my shoulders and then cinched the hip belt. Grunting, he zipped it so tight, the pressure took my breath away. Felt like a vice grip around my waist.

"That's not, um, very comfortable. It's not going to be like that the whole time, is it?"

As he fiddled with various straps and buckles, he laughed. "Yeah, all day, Mikey. It'll be even worse on day two."

He removed the pack, and I breathed a sigh of relief. Dipped a hand into my cargo pants and pulled out my hip flask for a sip.

He eyed me. "How much did you bring?"

"You said to plan for three days. So, only a couple bottles."

"You have water, too, right? I know an all-bourbon diet sounds like heaven to you, but it's death out here. Not even kidding right now."

I laid my hands on his shoulders. "Relax, Pugsley. It's going to be fine."

He frowned as he loaded his pack with all his gear, but he didn't say anything else on the subject. I pulled my duffel bag out of the back seat, to transfer the essentials to the backpack. I shoved clothes and necessary items in first. Made sure the three fifths of Evan Williams bourbon were well-wrapped. One inside a hoodie, one inside a pair of long underwear, and the last inside the sleeping bag.

Pug continued frowning at me as I lovingly wrapped my liquor before stowing it in my pack. I shrugged off his judgment; I'd only brought the absolute minimum. And, if one broke, it would be like issuing a DNR on me in the hospital.

Once we were both geared up, he helped me hoist the full pack onto me, and I nearly toppled over. The thing felt like wearing a professional wrestler on my back, trying to drag me to the ground.

Pug laughed at me. "We'll take breaks."

"I hope so," I said as I rolled my shoulders, trying to kill some of the pinching sensation at the base of my neck.

We faced the trailhead sign, and he removed two items from his pocket. He waited for a couple of day hikers to pass before he handed them to me. One, a trail map for Canyonlands National Park, Needles District. The park was so big, it had multiple maps. Hundreds of miles.

The other item was a photograph of Travis Pyuen, the man we were here to hunt. A man who had stolen twelve thousand dollars from our boss Gus and assaulted his wife in the process.

The man who needed to be held accountable for what he'd done.

CHAPTER FOUR

KANSAS - NOW

After the phone call with Gavin, I let myself sit in full panic mode for sixty seconds. Kept my eyes on the road, my hands on the wheel, flying along I-70 East.

Soon though, the panic ceases the upward trend. His visit is still five whole days away. There's absolutely no reason I can't get to Stillwater and back before then, doing everything I need to do along the way. It's simple math.

To center myself, I focus on the road, watching the mile markers tick by. I practice a little numbers game in my head when I see them. Add up the digits on each mile marker. Mile 106 is 1 plus 0 plus 6 which equals 7. It's hypnotic. After another minute or two, my heart rate is normal, and I feel a little better.

Back to the relentless task of driving.

Anyone who tells you Kansas is fun to traverse is lying

to your face. It consists of fields of wheat, grain silos, and the occasional cow. Lots of crosses along the side of the road, ringed with flowers. I assume those mark the spots where people have died from car accidents, but I've never stopped to check them out. Every once in a while, you'll see a billboard advising you to turn off to peruse home-made beef jerky or genuine venison meat.

None of these concern me. I'm driving, eyes forward. Boba Fett action figure perched on the dashboard. Music coming through the speakers, a playlist of hard tracks with guitars rumbling like train engines and beats fast enough to make me stomp my foot. No acoustic singer/songwriter stuff on a road trip. I need speed and purpose.

Hays, Kansas appears on the horizon long before I reach it because you can see forever in this state. Brick buildings and small-town streets. I exit the highway for a bathroom stop, and the strangest thing happens. As soon as I hit the brakes, the car lurches. I pump the brakes, and they're working fine, but the car seems to be fighting me somehow.

Then, there's a single sound from the engine, a wet cough. A sputter, another lurch, and the engine revs like it's not in gear. The temperature light creeps up and up until it nears the top, in the red.

I ease the speed down as I reach the bottom of the highway exit. A whiff of smoke pours from the engine. A puff of dark gray leaking out of either side of the car's hood.

"Don't panic," I say to the severed head of Boba Fett. "This is probably nothing. Just some normal engine thing with a slight hiccup I have no idea how to fix."

My first instinct is to pull it over to the side of the road and lift the hood. That's what a real man would do. But, the problem with that scenario is I know next to nothing about cars. I have vivid memories of being a teenager and my father showing me how to change a tire. That, I do know how to do. Every human has to know how to change a tire. But all the other car maintenance lessons my father tried to impart? They were evacuated from my brain to make room for other things that seemed important at the time, like lyrics and guitar chords to songs, plus vivid memories of hot girls from my high school.

The other reason I decide not to pull over is that a few hundred feet up the road, right next to a McDonalds, is a place named Zeke's Auto. Sign out front promising free tire rotation with an oil change, this week only.

Zeke's Auto feels like divine intervention.

The light turns green, and I gingerly press the gas. Smoke is continuously pouring out from under the hood now, black and smelly. Like demon horns sprouting from my poor little Camry. I'm wrestling with the steering wheel.

I have visions of the car exploding before I can drive it half a block to the auto shop.

"Come on, baby, just a little bit longer."

On the side of the road sits an old couple, lounging in

lawn chairs on the sidewalk, watching the street for no discernible reason. The man points at my car as I glide past, then he leans over and says something to his female counterpart.

I slide into the parking lot at Zeke's auto, a little shop with two garages, one empty, one with a mud-speckled Ford truck up on a lift. Two men in beige coveralls are underneath it, unscrewing something I can't see.

When I kill the engine in the parking lot, a gust of black smoke belches out from under my car hood and disappears into the air.

One of the two men under the truck tilts his nose up and sniffs, then he turns around, and his eyes jump wide when he sees my stinking carcass of a vehicle. He stands, wiping his hands on a towel slung over his shoulders. I can feel my face reddening and become suddenly and totally self-conscious of his judgment. Should have taken better care of my car.

I get out of the driver's seat as the man waddles over. He's large and round, with a beard that extends six inches below his chin, but is neat and trim on the sides.

He shoves out a hand, half-black with oil smudges. "Zeke."

"Micah." I'm still getting used to saying that instead of *Michael,* but it's easier now. I had a lot of practice in prison. Back then, though, it felt like pretend. Everything in prison is a certain degree of pretending. Out here, when I say my name, it feels like lying. Like I'm a spy.

"Looks like you got here just in time, Micah. That smoke coming out there is definitely *no bueno.*"

"I'm in kind of a hurry. Can you look at it now?"

Zeke looks back at the truck and then squints at me, sun highlighting his face and grime lining the wrinkles around his eyes. "Gimme about another hour on this truck, and then I can take a look. What I'll find under your hood, though, I have no idea, sir."

"What does that mean?"

Zeke shrugs. "May be nothing, or may be a whole lot of something."

A pulse of anxiety grips my chest. "Is there somewhere else I can take it? Somewhere nearby?"

"Sure," Zeke says, rocking back and forth on his feet. "There's a Midas over on thirteenth, but there's no way in hell you're going to operate this car right now."

"Excuse me?"

"You drive this thing one more inch, you might boil your engine. I don't think I could live with myself if I let you leave in this car and you explode on me."

A little nervous giggle escapes my lips. Exploding? Is he serious?

"Don't you worry, Micah, I'll take good care of her." He holds his hand out, flexing dirty fingers toward his chest. He wants the keys.

I open the door and snatch Boba Fett off the dashboard, then grip the keys. Metal presses into my palm.

Feels like I'm signing away my autonomy, willfully stranding myself in Kansas.

"Come back in about two hours," he says. "I'll know more by then."

I check the time on my phone. It's not game-over to lose a few hours, but I don't need this delay. Zeke doesn't care. He doesn't want me to explode, and I have no choice but to believe him.

With that, I drop the keys, and they thunk onto his palm. The smile on Zeke's face is supposed to comfort me, but I can feel the ache of powerlessness in my chest.

Why didn't I pay attention all those times my dad told me how to take care of cars?

Nothing I can do about it at this second.

Zeke pockets the keys and waddles back to the garage. I turn and survey the street. There's the McDonalds, a scrapbooking shop, a tire store, and a bar named *The Longmire Saloon*.

I promised myself no alcohol until I have the shoebox in my possession. Especially now that I have to deal with this car situation, having a drink is a bad idea. A very bad idea. Maybe I don't maintain a lot of hard moral standards, but I do not drive drunk.

So, I head across the street to the McDonalds and order an early lunch. While I wait for my burger and fries, I'm watching people traipse in and out of the saloon two doors down. Lots of cowboy hats and boots, some buckle bunnies, and a few older couples. The older couples interest me. Maybe the saloon serves lunch. I doubt all of these people are going in for alcohol because it's not even noon on a Monday.

A meager burger and limp french fries sit on the tray as it slides across the counter toward me. I don't want them. This meal will disappoint me. I'm sure of it.

Maybe I can go to the saloon and just order some food, no alcohol. Don't see what it could hurt to upgrade my burger.

I drop my tray full of food in the trash and head over toward the bar.

CHAPTER FIVE

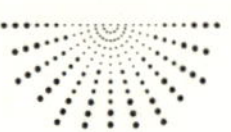

KANSAS - NOW

I open the door of the Longmire Saloon to find inside exactly what I expected: a shit-kicking bar full of country music and rednecks swilling beer. Peanut shells on the floor and the heads of dead animals on the walls. Not that I'm in a position to judge; I've spent more than my fair share of time in establishments such as this one. Out in rural Oklahoma, you rarely have a choice when you're thirsty.

I sidle up to the bar, and a bartender eases down to see me. She's a little younger than me, maybe twenty-five. She's white, with brilliant blue eyes and blonde hair braided down her back. Eyelashes a mile long. Her hands are lined with tiny cuts and bruises, like the mark of someone who works for a living. I can respect that.

"What can I get you?" she says.

"A menu, please."

She grins with only half her face, which strikes me as uncannily sexy, for some reason. Her working hands drop a laminated menu on the bar. Bright pictures of all the typical American pub fare. "Running a special on pork ribs today."

"Sure, that sounds great. I'll have that with fries."

"Coming right up, sugar. Anything to wet your whistle?"

My eyes travel across the selection of beer taps lining the bar. One beer should be fine, I think. I have a rule against drinking and driving, but I also have a sinking feeling I might not be driving anywhere today. "Budweiser draft."

She nods, and I feel guilty, but it's already been a hard day. I need to forgive myself. Once this is over and I'm back in Denver with the shoebox by my side, none of this will have mattered. Just a pit stop on the way to success. Hopefully.

While I'm waiting for my food, I spend time people-watching around the bar. It's not crowded. Maybe fifteen patrons total across the room. People eating, drinking, keeping to themselves.

One table in particular gains my interest, though. Three young men, all wearing flannel shirts, and Carhartt jeans. A dwindling pitcher on the table between them, no food. They're loud and brash and remind me of the sort of ruffians I used to squabble with in school. These guys are all too old to be in high school, but they do act like they're teenagers. A major topic of their conversation is some guy they don't like named Chester and all the particulars about why they don't like him. The list goes on for five minutes, often punctuated by raucous laughter about Chester's deficiencies. This is juvenile and dumb, but I shrug it off. I don't want to get involved.

But it's not until they turn their conversation to a woman they don't like that I can't tune them out any longer. The reason they don't like this woman is that she's apparently a slut. All three of the rednecks at the table have slept with her, and they toss insults about her left and right.

I know I should stop listening now and mind my own business because there's nothing I can do. It's not as if I can march over there, slam my beer on the table, and say, *you need to respect women, or I'm going to punch you in the face until you learn a lesson*. Maybe it'll make me feel better for a brief second. Probably, it won't, and it's not going to change their behavior.

They berated poor old Chester for about ten minutes. The conversation about this woman has now been going on for at least that long. My skin is crawling. The urge to throw my beer at them grows on me like an itch. A little at first. By the time I've finished my ribs and I'm on my third beer, their conversation is really bothering me. They won't stop degrading this poor girl.

And it's bothering the other patrons in the bar, too. The older couple I saw coming in here earlier is now throwing ugly looks at the rowdy crew. The bartender repeatedly frowns at them, but she's not actively doing anything about it, either.

No one is going to tell these punks to keep their voices down. Why is it falling to me?

I catch one of them scoping me out of the corner of his eye. I tilt my head away, back toward the mirror behind the bar, but it's too late. He stands. He's huge, at least six inches taller than me, with tree-trunk arms and stubby legs. A scraggly beard rims his jowls.

The bearded one struts across the room and stops next to the bar, facing me. My eyes are still forward, and I'm watching him in the mirror.

"You got a problem?" he says in a thick voice, like molasses. A lot of bass in his tone. He's hovering close enough that I could elbow him in the crotch, but I'm still hoping for a non-violent solution to this utterly dumb situation.

"Nope," I say. "No problem here."

"I saw you staring at us. Doing—what do you call it?—eavesdropping on our private conversation."

"That's not what was happening. I think you made a mistake."

The man leans in, and I can smell the cheap beer on his breath. A necklace dangles as he leans. A silver crucifix hanging from a chain. "Are you calling me a liar?"

"No," I say, eyes still forward, "I said you made a

mistake. It's not the same thing." I would love to add the word *dipshit* to the end of my sentence, but I refrain.

My restraint doesn't matter, though. He grabs my arm, just above the elbow. For a fleeting moment, I feel a lament. Lament about the sheer number of bar fights I've had in my life that have all begun like this, or something close to it. And, that I'm certain this won't be my last.

He slides one hand down, toward my wrist, and I know exactly what he's doing. I've done it too. He wants to twist my arm to tilt me off balance and ruin my leverage. Probably slam my head into the bar.

I'm not going to let him.

I jerk my arm back, freeing it from his grasp. Despite consuming three beers, I'm nowhere close to drunk. Not even buzzed. The redneck, though, sports bleary eyes. Unfocused. He's blitzed, and it shows.

I kick the barstool back as I swing up my other hand, cracking him in the jaw. He stumbles back, two steps, three steps, and he slips on a peanut shell. The back of his head smacks into a nearby table as his two friends stand up.

"Not inside!" howls the beautiful bartender. "Take it outside right this minute!"

It's too late for that. While the bearded redneck is lying on the floor, grunting and trying to roll over, the other two come rushing for me. One is closer, so I target him first. I spin, letting my hand gain momentum. It cracks against his jaw, which feels like a block of ice. For a moment, I'm jarred. Think my hand might be broken.

It's so surprising that I don't see the other one slip behind me. He wraps his hands around my arms, just below the armpits. Grip is solid, like steel. He cinches his arms together behind me, locking my arms behind my back. The tension in my shoulders makes me want to cry out, but I'm too busy trying to wriggle free.

The first one, rolling his jaw, raises his fists. I can't get away. He draws back and throws a punch into my gut. The air rushes out of me, and my abs tighten, making my lunch rocket from my belly, up into my throat. Everything goes woozy for a couple of seconds.

He's drawing back to punch again. Big smile, mouth full of yellow and black teeth. *Meth-heads.* Now, it all makes sense. I used to deal with angry Crankster Gangsters all the time back in my old job in Oklahoma.

As he starts his forward motion, I jab the heel of my shoe onto the toes of the guy behind me. He releases his grip on my arms, and I allow my body to crumple to the floor. I can feel air whoosh as the redneck's fist whiffs above my head, smacking his buddy in the chest. It's a bit of poetic justice.

Behind us, a shotgun cocks.

I jump up to my feet and catch the blonde out of my peripheral, lowering the barrel of the shotgun. Pointed in our general area, not at anyone in particular. But it gets their attention.

"I told y'all a million times not to bring this shit into the bar. If you gotta swing your dicks around, you are going to do it out—"

And I'm off before she can finish the sentence. Sights set on the front door, I don't bother to note where anyone else is. I'm solely focused on getting out into the street and away from this craziness. Twelve steps from my position to the door outside.

As I burst through the door, I squint down the street toward Zeke's Auto. Sun above beating down, a bright and clear blue-sky day. I see my car backing out of the garage, into the parking lot in front of the shop.

I pivot and sprint in that direction. Heart pounding, racing across the street and treading the grainy gravel under my feet.

Zeke steps out of my car, pinching the keys in his hand.

"What's the charge?" I shout as I near him in the parking lot.

He gives me a funny look. "Huh?"

I skid to a stop a few feet in front of him. "What's the charge?"

"Well, all it really took was some duct tape to get her going, but you're gonna wanna take that thing into—"

I yank out my wallet as I snatch the keys from his hand. "The charge."

"Sixty bucks for parts and labor."

I grasp three twenties and toss them, fluttering in the air and floating to the ground in front of him. When he bends over to pick them up, I yank the car door open and leap inside. Slam the keys in the ignition and throw it into reverse.

And as I back out into the street, I see those two rednecks rushing out of the saloon, toward their truck.

As soon as I start mine up, so do they.

CHAPTER SIX

UTAH - FOUR YEARS AGO

My shoulders and hips hurt as soon as Pug and I set out. From the first step past the Elephant Hill trailhead marker, it was like being squeezed around the middle. Plus, the pack jiggled left or right with each step. Side to side, side to side. I didn't know how I could hike for hours like this.

My hiking boots were covered with trail dust in less than a minute, and we'd barely gone two hundred feet. The uneven path cut up an incline between bushy trees on either side. The ground underneath was covered with a strange black substance, like a prickly layer on top of the pinkish dirt. This black substance seemed like it had infected everything within sight. I'd been contemplating it for ten or fifteen minutes.

"Pug. Wait up."

He turned, hands looped through his pack's shoulder

straps. Smiling, not even a little out of breath. As dapper as ever. "Sup?"

I pointed down at the strange earth. "What's up with this stuff?"

"Don't bust the crust," he said.

"Don't do what to the what?"

"It's cryptobiotic soil," he said. "A bacteria that grows out here. Careful with it. It's, like, illegal or something to step on it. Take only pictures and leave only footprints, Mikey."

"But not on the crust."

He grinned and sipped from his bottle before turning back around and continuing up the trail. "You got me there," he said, his voice bouncing off the surrounding rocks.

With a deep breath, I followed, sights on the ascent of the trail ahead. All around us, yellow and pink boulders cast shadows on the ground, which was sometimes rocky, sometimes like sandy beach at the ocean.

Bottles of bourbon in my pack clanked around, despite how well I'd wrapped them. And I was always conscious of the Springfield 1911 pistol in the top section of my pack. If Travis Pyuen made a sudden appearance, hopefully, I'd be able to whip out the pistol in time. I pictured him, gun in hand. Aiming it to kill me. Me, panting and exhausted, wearing a thirty-pound pack.

It would have made more sense for me to keep it in the back of my waistband, but I was more worried about butt-crack sweat. If I had to whip it out and the thing slipped from my hand, that would be no good, either.

A cluster of trail-running day hikers came from the opposite direction, toward us on the trail. We both pulled to the side, leaning against a boulder as big as a house. I relished the opportunity to push against it and relieve some of the weight from my shoulders. These no-body-fat trail runners whizzed by us, eyes forward, not acknowledging us at all.

After they'd gone, we both stood there, resting.

"So," I said, in between gasps, "how do we know for sure he's in Utah?"

"What do you mean?"

"I'm just saying, isn't it weirdly specific that Gus told us we would find this guy out here? How did he know Travis would be in this one national park in Utah, in this specific area of the park?"

Pug shrugged and continued on again. The hill came to a set of stairs carved into rock, between two sheer boulders blocking the view on either side. Pug grunted as we climbed. "I don't know how Gus knows anything. But if he says Travis is here, then he's here. And we keep poking around until we find him and get the money back. Anything less isn't going to cut it."

But then there was the other matter, that Travis had assaulted Gus' wife. He'd made no mention of specifically what to do about that, but the implication had been clear: Travis needed to be roughed up. Made to understand that someone like Gus wouldn't tolerate harm coming to his family. I expected Gus would want to see a picture of Travis with his face bloodied, or he wouldn't consider our mission a success.

I didn't relish the thought of doing that. Even if he deserved it.

The crest of the hill came into focus, and in a few more feet, we reached the top. My eyes opened wide at the valley below. Hundreds of what I assumed were the "needles": spires of multi-colored rock-like pieces of candy corn, jutting up from the earth, dotting the valley between the clusters of trees and wide-open flat spaces. Canyons and expanses of the pale pinkish-orange slick rock everywhere.

On the ground next to us sat a little pile of rocks. A cairn. One larger rock on the bottom, stacked with a pyramid of smaller rocks on top. A way-finder for which path to take next.

"This view is unreal," Pug said. "Seriously amazing."

I might have said the same thing if I weren't so troubled by the task in front of us.

CHAPTER SEVEN

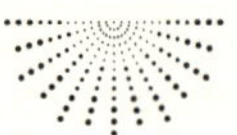

KANSAS - NOW

I hauled ass to Salina, continuing west along I-70. Hand and stomach aching from the brief squabble in the bar in Hays. While the injuries quickly settled into a low throb, my heart has not stopped pounding since I sprinted away from that sexy bartender with the shotgun.

I only saw the two rednecks in their Chevy truck once, and that was a few minutes after I left Hays. Maybe they tailed me for five minutes, ten minutes, thinking I'm a local and they would follow me home to kick my ass. But no way were they going to follow me for an hour or more. Wouldn't make sense.

But then, it occurs to me that they were drinking in a bar in the late morning, so it's not likely they have jobs they're missing out on.

Whatever. There's no way they're still back there, plotting my demise. Even though I've been checking the rearview compulsively every few seconds, the green Chevy I saw when I first left Hays has not made a reappearance.

The three beers quickly drain out of my system, and my foot thumps against the floor. This is not the auspicious and clandestine start I wanted for this jaunt to Oklahoma.

In Salina, I exit to I-135, to begin my descent south into Oklahoma. The flatlands of rural Kansas give way to the far-reaching limbs of suburbs of Kansas City and Wichita. Silos become buildings, and wheat fields morph into parking lots.

I'm nearing the little town of McPherson, and the maps app says I have about three hours to go. That should get me into Stillwater just in time for dinner, possibly Hideaway Pizza. I'd be wise to avoid Eskimo Joe's until after I've retrieved the shoebox. Too much temptation at the bar there.

Mere thoughts about Hideaway and Joe's fill me with emotions I have a hard time categorizing. Part nostalgia, part dread, part excitement, part shame. I'm not even sure which of those dominates, or which one will come up next in the continuous rotation.

Within a few minutes, the town of McPherson fades again. Turns to open lands, broad and seemingly infinite. My eyes flick one more time to the rearview, now out of habit more than a desire to check.

And I see a green Chevy Silverado, looming two cars back.

"You've got to be shitting me. That can't be the same car."

I look at Boba Fett, sitting on the dashboard, his pointy helmet facing me. He doesn't have shoulders, but he would have shrugged them if he did.

Can't be the same car. No way.

The car between us changes lanes, and the green Chevy accelerates. I can now see the two occupants inside, bobbing their heads to music, glaring at me.

It's them. I can barely believe it. I blink a few times, but their faces don't change. Two of the three rednecks I scuffled with at the bar are behind me, gaining on me.

No cars drive on the other side of the highway, nothing else behind us. I pass a sign indicating a rest stop up ahead in two miles.

The Chevy accelerates. Before I know it's happening, the truck contacts the back of my Camry. Just a bump, but the truck's massive size rocks my little car. I slam forward, and the seatbelt catches. My neck hurts instantly.

The grill of the Chevy bears down on me like a shark. Bumps me again, but not as hard, and the seatbelt doesn't catch me this time. A few more of those and they'll run me off the road.

The truck pulls back a few feet, then I hear it accelerate again. Screaming forward. I hit the gas, but don't have enough juice to escape, and their car hits me a third time. Lurch forward, neck strain.

I think about the duct tape holding together whatever it is Zeke fixed back at his garage. What if they jar it loose and strand me here? What if it explodes like Zeke said it could?

I have to deal with this, now.

I shift lanes and hit the brake to pull into the rest stop. The truck slows with me. As I enter the turn lane, I pop open the glove box and withdraw a screwdriver. I used to carry a gun every day, but since my incarceration and subsequent entry into Witness Protection, I haven't tried to acquire one. I don't think US Marshal Gavin Belmont would enjoy seeing my name pop up on a firearms background check.

So I palm the screwdriver and slow to the rest stop. Beads of sweat dripping down my back. This is not what I need right now, but I have to deal with it.

The rest stop is a stone building with two bathrooms, a picnic table with a shelter built overhead, and a small parking lot. Nothing but flat farmland in every direction.

I park behind it, on the far side, to keep prying highway eyes off me and my car. I slip the screwdriver into my back pocket as I step out and wait for them to park.

With no idea what I'm going to say, I have to hope I can talk my way out of this. Convince them it's not worth it to keep pestering me.

I'm praying they don't leap out of their truck with shotguns, but there's a good chance they'll be armed. But when they step out, they have nothing in their hands.

I let out a sigh of relief. Still, I keep my hand near the screwdriver. No idea if I can take them both on, but it might be my only choice. These two have proved to be entirely unpredictable so far.

As they step into view, I get a good look at their faces. The black-toothed one who'd punched me at the bar is taller, with a Kansas City Chiefs trucker cap and slender limbs. The other is short, with wavy black hair and a goatee.

"You have any idea what you did to Jake back there?" the tall one says. Fists balled at his side. Veins on his forearms popping.

"Who's Jake?" I say.

"He's the guy you sent into the table. Split the back of his head open."

I let my hand hang near my back pocket where the screwdriver sits, point facing down. Flex it a few times. "Doesn't seem you're all that concerned about him if you're here talking to me instead of taking him to the hospital."

Short one tilts his head forward and spits a jet of spearmint-flavored tobacco juice onto the gravel parking lot. "You're a smartass. You think you're better than us?"

"That has nothing to do with it. He walked over and attacked me first. I was defending myself."

"You're going to come back with us and apologize," the tall one says.

I shake my head. "Not going to happen. I have to be somewhere, and I'm on a deadline. If I go back to Hays with you, that messes up a whole lot of stuff I don't have time to explain to you."

Tall one's arm drifts toward the back of his pants, and I grip the handle of the screwdriver. He pulls out a Ruger SP101 revolver. Clean and shiny. Looks like it's never been fired.

"Bobby," the short one says, his hands out, defensively. "Bobby, what are you doing?"

Over his shoulder, I see a Kansas State Trooper vehicle driving along the highway. Panic strokes my insides.

"Put that away," I say.

"You going to make me?" he says and then points it up into the sky.

"Listen to me, you idiot, stow that gun right now. We're about to be in some serious shit if you don't listen to me."

Like a petulant child, he presses the trigger, muzzle pointed at the sky. The shot echoes. The state trooper's lights flip on, and the car slows to turn into the exit lane. Chirp of a siren. All of this is so predictable, I'm hardly surprised.

The two rednecks spin around as the trooper nears the rest stop.

I snatch my keys from my pocket and race toward the Camry. It takes me less than a second to reach my car, but a million thoughts rush through my head as I'm running. What happens if I'm arrested. What happens when Gavin finds out about it. What happens when my boss Frank finds out about it. Or, maybe even worse, what happens if I get dumped into the legal system, and one of my old employers finds out about it? I'm sure they must have people on the inside of the law, looking out for snitches like me. If that happens, my parents and my brother and sister are as good as dead.

Need to get out of here, now.

When I roll into my driver's seat, my brain screams at me that the car might not start when I turn the key. That I'm stuck. There's a lump in my throat, and I can barely swallow.

I jam the key in and crank it. The car does start. Grumbling, unhappy, but the engine turns over and kicks to life.

At this second, I see multiple events in the rearview: the two rednecks scrambling to race back to their truck. I can see the lights of the trooper's car, but not the car itself. With my car parked on the far side of the building, I'm shielded, at least for another second or two.

I floor the gas, flinging chalky gravel up into the air as the trooper pulls around the rest stop, blocking in the Chevy. There's only one cop car, so maybe I have a chance while he's occupied.

I peel out of the rest stop parking lot as the trooper exits his vehicle and the rednecks put their hands in the air. Did the trooper see me? Has he called in another car to chase me down the highway?

As I merge back onto I-135, I have no answers, so I keep my foot on the gas, trying to get to Oklahoma as fast as possible.

CHAPTER EIGHT

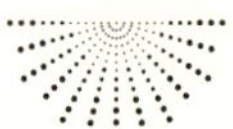

OKLAHOMA - NOW

For another hour, I drove and didn't see any cops or state troopers behind me. My eyes are red and itchy from staring at the rearview so many times. But, by now, my heart is starting to settle back into a normal rhythm.

I've probably burned a thousand calories by pumping my knee up and down. The heavy music helps.

When I cross into Oklahoma and note the welcome sign at the border, emotion floods me. Terror, because so many bad things happened here. Also, a little bit of warmth, because before the bad things, good things happened here, too. The balance of good and bad shifted significantly in the later years, but it wasn't always that way. I left a lot behind when I moved to Denver, (largely) against my will. Some things, I never want to know again. When my first WitSec handler told me I could never go home again, I spent the next week in prison trying to figure out how I felt about that.

And now, here I am, like an idiot, leaping back into a trough of muck to dive head-first into all that history and root around in it. I have to keep in mind why I'm doing all this: the shoebox. To preserve the last remnants of Michael McBriar, a man who no longer exists.

As I pass the exit for Ponca City, a strong urge to turn around gnaws at me. That my old self isn't worth saving. That the bad memories outweigh the good, I should let them go, and it's not worth risking allowing Gavin to find out about it.

But no. I have plenty of time until my handler's visit to Denver. As long as I have no more run-ins with the police, there should be no trouble.

And as soon as I think that, an Oklahoma Highway Patrol car comes racing north along I-35, lights and sirens blaring. Right in my direction, hurtling toward Kansas.

My heart bumps so hard, I don't know if I can take it. I grip the steering wheel and blink a few times, tired eyes dry and scratchy. If I'm pulled over, this is the end. Back to prison. There's no more future for me, regardless of the name on my license.

Maybe this was a terrible idea.

But the patrol car zooms past, the lights dim, and the sirens fade into my rearview. Not after me. After someone else.

I need to rest. Soon. I've been through enough already

for one day. But, I know I'm not done yet. I have to recover the shoebox tonight because it's too risky to leave it for tomorrow. Gotta be conscious of the timeline. And, no way will I attempt a retrieval during the day.

In another thirty minutes, I'm nearing the exit for Stillwater. A new itch burns at me, to continue on past this exit and divert to Oklahoma City. To see the place where it all went down. The Freedom House, the building we used as our base of operations. The beginning and the end of my career in the service of those people who ruined my life.

Does the Freedom House still stand? Have they torn it down? The latter option wouldn't surprise me.

I also wonder if I have any family living in the area. My sister has moved to the mountains of Colorado, but I'm not sure about my brother and my parents. By the conditions of my arrangement with the government, I've avoided keeping tabs on them.

If they're still here, will they be happy to see me, or will they turn their backs?

These are the questions I'm asking myself as I near Highway 51.

"Boba, tell me I'm being an idiot."

You're being an idiot, he says from his perch on the dashboard.

"Thank you," I say as I flick on my turn signal and slow toward the exit for Stillwater. The idea of revisiting those old haunts is a fantasy. Pure fiction. My parents and siblings think I'm dead, for their own protection. Showing up at their door so I can steal a taste of nostalgia is a selfish and dangerous option.

It never will be safe to come here, ever again. Oklahoma is my home, but it's not. It's nothing but a place where my former self lived, and there's nothing I can do to change that fact.

And then, after a few more minutes on the highway, I'm approaching Stillwater, Oklahoma. Small-town gas stations and the stink of pig farms. Long-abandoned oil well pumpjacks that sit atop the earth like birds pecking for bits of food.

A parked cop car looms large on the side of the road near the edge of town. As I pass by it, two officers inside track me, their mirrored sunglasses reflecting the setting sun into my eyes.

CHAPTER NINE

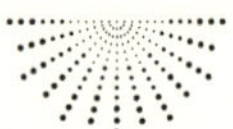

OKLAHOMA - NOW

It's seven pm in Stillwater, Oklahoma. My belly is full of Hideaway Pizza, and I'm sitting in my car in the parking lot across the street from my old apartment. At least they didn't tear it down to put up a new building, as fear-mongering Boba Fett suggested earlier.

Still here, still untouched. A testament to the beginning of the end of my old life. Also, the end of the end of my old life.

It's hard to contain these feelings. So much happened there. It's hard not to look at that building and think of all the mornings I woke up inside it, with no idea of where I'd been the night before. Hungover, barely able to think due to the pounding in my head. And then, the confusion wouldn't get any better when I would find bloodstains on my shirt and fewer bullets in my Beretta's magazine than I expected to find.

It's a lot to take in, sitting here.

The building is two stories, a single apartment on each floor. There is one set of wooden stairs leading up to the second-floor apartment. A wooden walkway out front, with a single window overlooking that, and another in the kitchen on the side. There is no outside access to the window in the kitchen; it's a straight shot from that window to the ground. No roof access. So, I'm either going in the front door or the window into the living room via the walkway. The inside layout is incredibly simple: it's one large room with a tall wooden divider halving the place into living room and bedroom. This divider reaches from the floor to about a foot below the ceiling. The kitchen is along the wall opposite the divider, and there is a single bathroom in the back.

There's no stealthy way in. Open the front door or slide in a window, and anyone inside that apartment will hear me if they don't immediately see me. It's tiny inside there.

My throat burns for a drink, and I'm tempted to walk down to the corner and duck my head into Willie's for a quick beer. Hell, I'm more than tempted. I've been thinking about it constantly since I first saw the edge of town. Since I first felt that Stillwater sensation this afternoon.

But I can't do that yet. I need to sneak in there and recover my shoebox. All other concerns can wait.

The problem is the *two* people inside the apartment.

I've seen a white guy hovering near the living room window, and a black guy leaving the apartment to shuffle down to the parking lot a few times. He's taken things out of a car and then returned to the apartment. This has happened four times in the hour I've been sitting in this parking lot, watching.

If they're students, they might be in there all night. It's a school night, and not even a going-out school night like Ladies Night or Thirsty Thursday.

I can wait until tomorrow and try it again, but I don't like pushing another day closer to the deadline for Gavin's visit to Denver. I want to be back in town with plenty of cushion. Also, when I asked Frank for a couple days off work, I was vague about how much time. I don't want to linger out here for days on end and disappoint him. The old ex-cop has a deep, fatherly look when he frowns. It's hard to endure.

So, the retrieval has to be tonight. No other option.

While I'm waiting, I get restless. Have to stretch my legs. I want to feel those old fun feelings of roaming around Stillwater again, so I leave the car and take deep breaths of the atmosphere in this college neighborhood.

Outside, Stillwater has no particular smell, and the sky has nothing familiar in its appearance. It's all faceless, small-town America. A little more humidity, compared to Colorado. The sky has more stars than Denver, but that's to be expected, this far from a major city.

Part of me thought it might feel comfortable to be here, despite the initial panic when I first drove in. But it doesn't feel like anything now. It's cold. I had friends here, but I can't go to them. I'm alone.

As I stroll along a street, a small orange cat drops from a nearby fence and pads over toward me. Meowing as it slinks along the grass of someone's front lawn. I sink to a knee, which makes the kitty move faster on a collision course. When I stick out a hand to pet it, the cat angles toward me, crashing up against my hand. Smushing its body into my forearm, forcing me to run my fingers along its slender frame.

"That's Jasper," says a male voice.

I look up to see a young guy, maybe twenty. Brown-skinned, with spiky and short dreadlocks. His accent is not American, but I can't place it. Jamaican, or another island somewhere in the vicinity.

"Jasper?"

He nods. "That's right, man."

Jasper continues to weave back and forth against my extended arm, crashing into me with each pass. "Is he your cat?"

The kid shakes his head. "He nobody's cat. Belongs to the neighborhood. Sleeps where he pleases and visits who he like."

"I see."

The kid opens a pack of cigarettes. Parliaments, the

same brand my best friend smoked. As he pops a cigarette into his mouth, his face darkens. Eyes dim. "He belong to all of us, so don't you think about taking him. Dig?"

"I wasn't going to. No need to be snippy about it."

"Good, good." With that, the kid struts on past me, lighting up his smoke as he saunters down the sidewalk. Jasper the cat trots after the kid, and they both eventually turn at the next street.

What an odd exchange.

I check the time on my phone and head back to my car for more sitting and watching. At nine, the black guy leaves the apartment with his keys in hand. He trundles down the wooden stairs, making them shake. This sight brings a smile to my face. I clearly remember how rickety those wooden steps are. Seems the jerk of a landlord has done nothing to improve the place.

The black guy slips into a Prius and makes an exodus from the parking lot. One person inside now.

I entertain a quick fantasy of breaking in and overpowering the guy, but that's crazy. Hurting or terrorizing some innocent person just because I'm in a hurry isn't in my plans. I don't want to hurt anyone at all. That's what the old me would do, back when I didn't care about being a bulldozer, crashing through everyone's lives. I'm trying to be a little more conscious now.

Can't bust in with force. Not an option.

No, my best bet is to wait until the lights go out and

then sneak in through the window by the walkway. I can see from here it's the same, single-pane window with no lock as when I lived here. I'll slide it up, drift inside, and then access the ceiling panels from there.

This will be easy.

CHAPTER TEN

OKLAHOMA - NOW

I wait until the lights have been out for an hour, and then I start my car and exit the parking lot next to my old building. I pull the car around to the corner of 4th and Hester, to put a little distance between my vehicle and the crime I'm about to commit. That's my old paranoia looking out for me. If I do get caught and arrested, the last thing I want is for them to impound my vehicle. Knowing the cops in this town, they'll do everything they can to screw me.

Now a block away, I creep back on foot, but try not to look like I'm creeping. Hands in my pockets, head up, walking at a normal pace. I'm meandering down 4th, watching the college kids on their front porches, listening to music and sipping beers. Six years ago, that was me. Before I flunked out of school, that is.

Before I became deeply involved with a group of people so sinister that I had to become a completely new person to escape them. And the only living remnants of that person are in a stupid little shoebox, hidden in the ceiling tiles in this building in front of me.

No random cats or Jamaican dudes out right now to bother me. Just this town, my anxiety, and a mission I have to complete as soon as possible.

Near the apartment building, I take care to notice any lingering pedestrians or lookers on porches. It's dark out, few streetlights, so I'm confident I'm in the shadows. I'm wearing jeans and a gray t-shirt, so not exactly master-level stealth here, but it could be worse.

In the parking lot of my old apartment, so many memories come flooding back. I wonder which government employee returned to clean up the apartment after the whole debacle. After the chaos and before the trial, I stayed in a safe house, far from here. Didn't have a chance to clean it up properly. In the closet, I kept all the boxes from the seemingly infinite number of beers I drank here. Called it the "dead beer storage." How many thousands of bottles and cans had I consumed in this sad little room above me?

I shake my head to clear my thoughts. Reminiscing needs to take a back seat. As I slink up the stairs, I keep my footfalls as light as possible, mindful of the rickety steps.

At the top, I lean to get a glimpse into the living room

window. It's dark, an LED on a coffee pot in the kitchen the only illumination available.

For a moment, I entertain the idea of knocking on the door. Simply asking the guy if I can have my shoebox back. Maybe the resident inside will be totally cool and ask no questions. Or maybe he'll say no, turn me away, and then search the apartment for it himself. He finds it and hands it over to the cops. Or, if he doesn't find it, I'll still have to break in later to steal it. And, he'll have seen my face and can report it to the police.

No. It has to be this way. This is ugly, and I hate it, but it has to be this way. This is something the old me would have done without even thinking about it.

I mean, I'm going to do it anyway tonight, but my guilt should count for something, shouldn't it?

Against the window, I press both hands onto the glass. Push up, and it rattles a bit while sliding. I pause, holding my breath, listening for movement. The apartment is so small, I can hear the occupant breathing on the other side of the divider. Slow, steady, even breaths. Definitely asleep. Can't see him, but he sounds like he's out.

His breathing doesn't change, so I push the window up higher. I lean in to see if there's anything to use on the other side as a cushion, like a couch or a table. There's nothing there, only blank space. He's set a couch against the divider and a TV in the corner, perpendicular to the window. No other furniture to speak of. The room isn't big enough to accommodate much.

If I go in headfirst, I'll tumble onto the floor, and that will be so loud, I might as well shoot pistols in the air. So, I need a better plan. Easy, quiet, and quick.

What I do instead is lean against the wooden rail on the walkway outside the apartment and step my feet up the wall. Bracing my hands behind me, extended. I stick my feet inside the window and then push myself away from the railing, slipping my lower legs and then knees into the window. Stretched out, completely vulnerable. I can get all the way up to my thighs before my arms strain against the railing. I push each of my knees to opposite ends of the window to brace them, then let go of the railing. For a moment, my abs are doing a hundred percent of the work to keep me aloft.

I reach forward and grab the corners of the window to hold my upper body in place, then I release the grip with my knees and slip inside the window.

My feet touch the floor, and then I let go of the window. I'm inside. Out of breath from the silent exertion. That smell of dank carpet and old plumbing hits my nostrils, and it's like coming home. Overwhelming. I want to sink to the floor and heave a few deep breaths until the feeling normalizes, but there's no time for that.

A distinct memory hits me. Me and my best friend, not long after we took the trip to Utah to confront Travis Pyuen, the man we'd been tasked to hunt. But, of course, what we found there turned out to be something completely different. After the endless trip driving home, both of us battered and bruised, we sat in my living room and drank a twelve-pack between the two of us. Not saying a word about it. Wanting to squelch the awful experiences we'd accumulated on the trip, but finding it nearly impossible.

I blink again. Have to focus.

The shoebox is in the ceiling panels right above the wooden room divider, dead center in the room.

I stand on top of the couch as something catches the corner of my eye. A cat, strutting around the divider. It's a long-haired thing, like a fur ball with two yellow eyes. Not the same cat I saw outside, but this creature could be its cousin. I don't remember Stillwater being so overrun with cats.

It sits at the edge of the kitchen, staring at me. Better than a guard dog, I suppose. Still, if it mewls at the stranger in its house, that's no good, either. Everyone will be happiest if I'm in and out without waking the sleeping guy.

The divider in the center of the room doesn't go all the way up; about a foot of space separates it from the ceiling. So, I latch onto the top and pull myself up. The cat's eyes track me, sitting in silent judgment in the kitchen.

Now, I'm staring down to the other side of the divider at a young guy sleeping on a futon. He's on his back, mouth open. One arm above his head, the other pointed down, like he's posed within a crime scene chalk line.

I use one hand to maintain balance on the divider, and the other to push the ceiling tile. It raises up an inch, then I slide it over, onto the adjacent tile.

My hand reaches around in the dark, fumbling over each square inch. Then it bumps against something, sending my heart into high gear. I tap it and can hear shuffling inside the object.

There it is. My shoebox.

Still here.

It's a tan box with a green top. I think it once housed a pair of generic white tennis shoes.

I reach out to pull it closer, and it's just a little beyond my reach. I strain, leaning over the divider. Barely getting a finger on it. The guy below me snorts, then rolls over onto his side.

I realize I've been holding my breath, so I inhale and let it out, easy. Then I lean forward again, snag the shoebox by one corner, and pull it back to me.

I have it. It's in my hand.

That's when I hear a car door shut outside.

My body freezes in place. Is someone coming? It could be in the next parking lot over. Or, the downstairs neighbor, maybe?

It's probably someone in the next parking lot.

Either way, the clock is ticking. Have to finish what I started and get the hell out of here. I set the shoebox on top of the divider so I can replace the ceiling panel. Then I clutch the shoe box under my arm and slide back down to the couch.

Outside, the steps rattle. Someone is coming upstairs. It's the roommate. Has to be.

I descend from the couch and consider my options. Nothing good comes to mind. A figure passes in front of the living room window. The black guy; the other roommate.

He's here. I'm out of time.

I race through the living room, toward the kitchen window. The cat hisses and skitters away from me, banging into the fridge. Guy in the bedroom sits up and utters some nonsensical sound that comes out like a question, but not as an actual word.

The front door opens.

I power forward, head first, into the kitchen window. My neck strains when the top of my head smacks into it. Glass crackles around my temple, shattering. The sound fills my ears as my head pushes through it.

Next thing I know, I'm falling, air whiffing by my face.

But it's over quickly. The ground rushes up to meet me. Dirt enters my mouth as my shoulders and arms connect first. Like being slapped across the entire front of my body.

My frame crumples, my arms folded underneath me and my legs flying up in the air. My lower half twists, then topples, so I'm doing an ugly kind of somersault on the ground.

For a second, I can't open my eyes. Can't move anything. Then I heave in a breath, and I can feel my limbs again.

I shake my head and sit up. Nothing feels broken. The shoebox is on the ground next to me, the top off, but the contents are still inside.

Above my head, the two guys shout. The apartment light flicks on. One of them leans out the broken window, and I turn to look up. I can see him, but it's dark down here. No lights on the side of the building, so I should be invisible to them.

"Sorry," I say as I get to my feet. "I'm really sorry about the window."

"What the hell are you doing?" the guy shouts.

But I don't answer him. My legs are churning, and now I can feel where I'm injured. Both of my hips hurt and my knees throb like someone has whacked them with a baseball bat a few times.

But I ignore the pain. I press forward, racing through the alley, back toward Hester Street. Heart pumping, chest heaving. The contents of the shoebox thrash around, clutched under my armpit.

I hold it tight. After everything I've been through to get my prize, it's not going anywhere. Ever again.

Guilt over breaking their window weighs on my head. But aside from the brief upset they'll feel, it won't cost them a dime. The landlord will replace it. And if they have the same asshole landlord I had when I lived here, I won't feel bad about that, either.

One minute later, I empty out onto Hester, and there's my Camry, but something is wrong. The hood and the trunk lid are both up. I'm positive I didn't leave it that way.

I slow to a walk, adrenaline rushing through me, making me feel like I'm over-caffeinated. Smells like oil and gasoline. Is that real?

I glance around as I approach the car, but there's nothing odd there. In the trunk, I check the spot by the spare tire, and it's gone. The thousand dollars in emergency money I had stashed in the wheel well is therefore also missing.

"Shit."

I've been robbed.

But then, I take a step back and note that the two rear tires have been slashed. When I round the car, I find the two front tires have also been slashed. And when I look under the hood, all the various cables and lines in the car have been either cut or removed. My car battery is missing, as well as my spark plugs. Someone didn't just sabotage my car, they flayed it.

This is more than a robbery.

There are puddles underneath. One of oil, one of washer fluid, one of gasoline. There are other fluids mixed in there I don't recognize.

This is not good. My car is dead. If my emergency

money is gone, I have about twenty dollars left in my thin wallet.

And then, when I lower the hood, it all makes sense. There, on the windshield of my Camry, is the splat of a spearmint-flavored tobacco juice spit stain.

Those god damn Kansas rednecks found me.

PART II

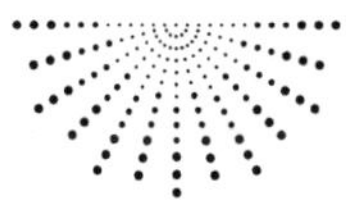

HERE COMES POPPA BEAR

CHAPTER ELEVEN

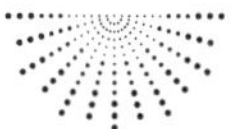

UTAH - FOUR YEARS AGO

We made it to Chesler Park right around lunchtime. Had seen hardly any people along the trails, maybe because it was a weekday in mid-Spring and the weather hovered somewhere between *cold-as-hell* and *barely tolerable.* I'd expected, since Utah was desert, for the days to be hot and dry and sweaty. Maybe I should have done some research.

As we descended through the series of rock formations into Chesler, the scope of it amazed me. A vast, flat valley, surrounded by hundreds of needle spires like multicolored fingers jutting from the earth. Grassy fields populated the valley, with a single cluster of rock spires in the middle.

As soon as we reached flat land, I shed my pack and collapsed against the nearest rock. Neck, shoulders, hips, and quads all burning. The back of my shirt was drenched in sweat, and I shivered as soon as my pack separated from my back.

As I grunted and struggled to free a water bottle from the side pouch of my pack, Pug tossed a sad frown at me.

"What are you, thirty-five?"

Panting, I gulped some water. "No, jerk. I'm not a hiker, and I may be a teensy, tiny bit out of shape. This is all new to me."

"But isn't it amazing?" he said, sweeping his hiking poles in a circle. "The clean air, the rocks, the open space and big-ass blue skies? It's like an alien world out here."

I nodded up at the wide-open blue above, larger than anything I could remember seeing. One patch of puffy clouds sat in the sky. Otherwise, it was untouched. "It's unreal."

I had memories of family trips with my brother, sister, and parents, piling into the family car and spending endless hours traversing the flat landscapes of Oklahoma to find some place interesting. How, as a little kid, the whole process of a family trip had seemed so magical. The views in places like the rocky mountains or the Grand Canyon, how they had been almost too big for me to comprehend.

But this was different. All I had to do then was sit in the car and not fight too much with my brother and sister. Today, I had *earned* this view by slugging a backpack full of gear all this way.

Pug shuffled over next to me so we were facing the

same direction, then took out his phone. He snapped a quick picture and then showed it to me. Him, smiling, as debonair as always. Me, mouth drooping, looking like I'd run a marathon. I had no interest in seeing that picture again, for sure.

"The girl from Stonewall the other night?" he asked as he lit up a Parliament cigarette.

"Yeah?"

With a sly grin, he said, "what happened?"

I shrugged, but he wagged a finger. "Nope. You don't get to weasel out of this one, Mikey. Did you bump uglies with her?"

I wanted to protest, but I couldn't keep a straight face. "Yeah, we had some fun back at my place. At least, I'm pretty sure we did."

"Unbelievable. You were so drunk, I couldn't believe she left with you. She was holding you up as you stumbled around the bar."

I stood and waved my hands over my body, highlighting the merchandise. "When you look like this, it's hard to resist."

"And she was okay with your shitty little apartment behind the plasma center?"

"I don't think she was paying much attention to the inside of my apartment. If you know what I mean."

Pug liked to hear about every detail of my exploits, but I was honestly not a kiss-and-tell sort of guy. Those random, sticky one night stands after episodes at the bar were a rarity in my world. The truth was that I didn't like bringing girls back to my place. I didn't like explaining that I lived in a college town, but I'd flunked out of college and had stuck around for the next few years like a townie, still bumming around keg parties at age twenty-four.

And I didn't like explaining that I worked for a group of Mexicans who were into something shady, probably. I didn't know exactly what that shady thing was because I'd never bothered to ask. I suspected illegal sports betting and underground casinos, or maybe loan sharking. There was always plenty of cash around. I showed up when and where I was told and did the things they asked me to do. Usually drunk, so I didn't have to think about it too much.

Either way, I couldn't explain my employment situation to most normal people.

Pug ground out his cigarette onto the sole of his shoe, stuck it in his pocket, and nodded at my pack. It rested on the ground like a tired dog. "I do know what you mean, you lush. Let's get going."

"I thought we were here. At our destination?"

"We are, Mikey, but we can't drop our shit and pitch the tent wherever we feel like. We have a designated spot." He lifted one finger and pointed it over my shoulder. "Our campsite is a ways around the valley."

I sighed, trying not to pout.

"Come on," he said, "don't puss out on me just yet."

We donned our packs, and I let Pug lead since he knew everything already. We traversed around the interior of the spires ringing the park. On our right, rock walls stretched fifty feet in the air, occasionally cut by boulders varied enough to allow room for climbing. On our left, the vast open space of grass intermingled with trees and shrubs.

After ten minutes of slogging through the grassy interior, I spotted something up ahead. A tree with a large backpack hanging from one of the lower branches. I grabbed Pug's arm and pointed, and he changed direction toward the little space next to a collection of boulders.

As we neared the area, I noted a camp stove on the ground as well as a tent erected under the shadow of the tree. The thought occurred to me to drop my pack and arm myself with the Springfield, but we had no reason to think this was Travis' campsite. Unless we found him or his wallet, this could be anyone's.

But, it was the first campsite we'd seen all day. That fact alone seemed strange.

Pug set his pack next to the tree, and I followed him. He unzipped the backpack hanging from the branch and rifled through the contents. While he did that, I opened the tent. Explored a blue rucksack filled with clothes. Men's clothes, for sure. No women's clothes anywhere, and everything in the collection was a size 32, so that suggested there was only one person here. The tent didn't seem big enough for two people, anyway.

"Got anything?" Pug said.

I crawled back out of the tent. "Not really. You?"

"A backpacking permit for seven nights, but I can't read the signature."

I joined Pug as he held out the sheet of paper. The name at the bottom was a meandering scrawl, too scratchy to read.

"What do you think?" he asked.

"I don't know. That first word could be Travis, I guess. Or it could be Stephen or Robert or Frank. I'm not a handwriting expert."

He stared at it again, moving it slowly toward and away from his face, squinting. "Shit."

"Did you think we'd just stumble on him out here?"

He shrugged. "I wasn't sure what was going to happen. But since we've seen, like, four or five other people total all day long, this is the first lead we've got."

"I dunno, Pugsley. We could find a spot nearby to hide and wait, I guess. See if he comes back."

I surveyed the nearby area. Out into the valley, there wasn't much to hide behind, except for a few scattered trees. "But that might be tricky."

Before he could respond, a whistling sound filled my ears. A split second later, I noticed something out of the corner of my eye. A dark object zipping through the air.

The rock cracked Pug on the side of his head before I could open my mouth to warn him. And then, as I spun to find where it had come from, another rock hit me in the forehead. My eyes shut involuntarily, pain splicing my head like a knife wound. My knees buckled from the surprise of it, but I held out my hands to keep myself upright.

When I opened my eyes, a figure leaped down from the rocks to our right. A muscular Asian man, clad in long underwear. Big, chunky biceps and a v-shaped back that angled down to a slim waist. This guy was a beast of a man. Like a firefighter from a calendar.

I turned back toward my pack, thinking I'd unzip the top and retrieve my pistol.

Something hard smacked me in the back, and I toppled a couple steps. Barely able to keep myself standing after the force of the blow knocked me forward. I turned to see Travis' leg retract as he lashed out at Pug with a backhand. This behemoth in his underwear was lightning quick and obviously strong. He landed three punches into Pug's gut before I managed to stop myself from falling into the dirt. Pug, who was one of the toughest guys I knew, had no answer for Travis' fists.

I spun and raced toward him as he continued to pummel Pug. Made a fist with my right and planted a foot. I launched my fist into Travis' side. When it connected, I felt the solidness of his abs, like punching a rock. He didn't even react when I hit him with everything I had in me.

He swept a hand back, smacking me against the jaw. I spun, stumbled, and my head connected with a rock on the ground.

Then, blackness.

CHAPTER TWELVE

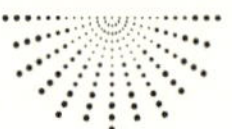

OKLAHOMA - NOW

I didn't want to sleep in the car because of the puddle of oil and gasoline festering below it. Didn't even want to attempt to start it up, for fear of tearing me (plus half the neighborhood) into pieces. I'd rather not go out in a blaze of glory. At least, not like that.

Instead, I popped into Willie's to have some drinks. The bartender I used to flirt with wasn't there, and I didn't ask after her because I didn't want to converse with anyone more than necessary. I clutched my shoebox tight and downed tequila shots with Dos Equis chasers. Stared at the shoebox, not opening it. Held it close, like an infant.

A few hours later, I stumbled over to Theta Pond on campus and found a tree to nestle underneath. With all the various aches and pains resulting from my jump out of the window, I was glad to find a soft spot of grass to rest my head.

As I sleep, I dream of being confined in a small space. On my belly, crawling, trying to escape. It's a cave or a tunnel or some sort of shaft, like an air conditioning duct. But, it's underground. I know that much. I can't see well enough because there's not enough light. All I know is that the tunnel around me will collapse if I don't move. Push forward. Do it now, or I might die in here. But something is holding me back. I can reach out with my hands and arms, but my legs stay behind me, rooted in place. Stretching, stretching, unable to bring my upper and lower torso along at the same speed.

A nearby conversation filters into my dream, first as people talking in the tunnel, and then, in that space between awake and asleep. Not in a tunnel. On the ground, in real life.

The sun warms my face for a moment and then disappears. I open my eyes, thinking maybe it's cloudy. But no. Instead of clouds, I find two campus police officers standing over me, blocking out the sun. Hands on hips, large sunglasses, handcuffs and revolvers and stun guns hanging from their belts.

"Good morning, sir. What's in the box?"

The cop on the left points to the shoebox, which I've been using as a pillow.

I sit up and both the cops take a step back. Hands out in front of their chests. They think I'm dangerous. "Shoes."

"Mind if we take a look?"

"Yes, I do mind."

"Sir, have you been out here all night?"

My brain is foggy. Options of what to say come to mind, but they're all too snarky. I don't want to piss these guys off. Verbally attacking the police is almost as bad as physically attacking them. "My wife kicked me out late last night, and I was too tired to find a place to sleep."

"Is that why you're not wearing a wedding ring?"

I look up, and the cop on the right shifts, letting the sun shine again. I squint against it. "Yes, that's why."

"And you brought your shoes with you."

"Yes, I did."

The cops share a quick look, then the one on the left sighs. He leans over to the other one and whispers something. After a moment, the other one nods.

"If we see you out here again, we're going to haul you down to the station. Campus is not a place for you to sleep out under the stars. You got that?"

"Yes."

And, then, they turn and march away. Within a few seconds, they're gone. And that's it. I can't believe it. For the first time in my history with this shitty town, I've had an interaction with the police that didn't end with me being dragged away in handcuffs, or worse.

I rub my eyes and look around, to make sure I'm where I think I am. Yep, I'm in Stillwater, Oklahoma. Home of the Oklahoma State University Cowboys, plus some bars and restaurants and not a lot else.

My stomach grumbles, and I set out on the twenty-minute walk to Shortcakes. Along the way, I detour onto Hester Street to check the status of my Camry. It's no longer there, which doesn't surprise me. I parked the car away from the apartment so it wouldn't be at risk for impound, but someone towed it anyway. Of course.

I wonder if the guys from the apartment called the police. Because if they reported a crime, and my car is somehow tied to it, that could cause trouble. The car is registered to me. Maybe the smart thing to do would be to call it in as stolen. But, if I do that and it gets around to Gavin Belmont, is he going to believe someone stole my car in Denver and then drove it all the way to Stillwater, Oklahoma, where I lived before I joined Witness Protection? That would be too big a coincidence for him to swallow.

But, my registration and insurance info are both on little slips of paper in the glove box. Eventually, someone will tie that car to me. My best hope is that it will sit in an impound lot for a few days before anyone gets around to searching it. By then, maybe I'll be back in Denver and will have thought of a much better reason why and how it got here.

So, I decide to do nothing, for now. I have to focus on how I'm going to get this shoebox home, or none of the rest of it matters. First, breakfast, then I'll solve all my other problems.

For fifteen more minutes, I shuffle along the road toward Shortcakes, shoebox under my armpit. Just a guy and his cardboard box, on a mission for some eggs and hash browns. I have so little left in my wallet, that's about all I can afford.

I take a detour along Duck Street, for pure nostalgia reasons. There's the yellow house where Garth Brooks lived at one point. We used to go over there for parties, sometimes. Long after Garth had moved out, of course, but the house was legendary. My friend Brent would stand in the kitchen and say things like, "Garth Brooks used to eat Pop Tarts right here, dude," and then we would giggle uncontrollably, both of us almost too drunk to stand. Not that we were Garth Brooks fans. It's amazing the things that crack you up when you're twenty and so full of alcohol it's coming out of your pores.

Ten more minutes to Shortcakes, and I'm working up a sweat by the time I get there. And when I see the little rectangular diner, something inside catches my eye. My jaw drops.

It's him.

Through the window, I can see one of the two rednecks who rammed into my car. The shorter one, with the black hair and the goatee. Not the one who pulled the gun and fired a round into the sky at the rest stop. The one who seemed to have some modicum of sense.

He's alone at a booth for two, shoveling grits into his face.

I duck behind a dumpster across the street and watch him. He's staring at his phone, eating. Only one plate on the table. He looks like hell, with his dark hair mussed and wearing what appears to be the same clothes from yesterday. I'm not sure about that last point, but they do look similar.

Eating alone at a booth for two. Where's the other one?

I wait a few minutes to see if the taller one joins him, but he doesn't. This redneck is here alone. And now, I note the lack of Chevy Silverados in the parking lot.

He came from Hays down to Stillwater in a different car? What the hell is going on here? It's not all that surprising to encounter him here; Stillwater is tiny, and everyone loves Shortcakes. Naturally.

He was here last night to mess up my car, but why is he alone? It's bothering me, and I can't get over it. I have to know.

In another couple minutes, the redneck wipes his mouth and stands up. Signs a credit card slip on the table and then heads toward the front door.

I stash the shoebox under the dumpster and cross the street. Fists balled, trying to shake the last remnants of sleep from my brain. Need answers.

In the parking lot, the redneck walks toward a little Honda Civic, keys out. Rental car sticker on the back of it. As he's fiddling with his keys to find the unlock button, I come up behind him. Snatch him by the wrist and jerk as hard as I can to move him away from the front of the diner. Beyond any prying eyes. My gaze flicks to the windows of the diner, and no one seems to pay any attention to us.

As I drag him, he's trying to get his feet underneath him, but I don't give him that chance. I jerk on his arm as I increase my jog to a run, and it's all he can do to keep from falling to the cement below us.

Around the side of the restaurant, I whirl him around and force him against the brick exterior of the building. Press my forearm into his throat while I pin him. I use both my free arm and my hips to keep him flat against the building and unable to wriggle free.

"Surprise, asshole," I say. "Bet you thought you wouldn't see me again."

He squawks something, but with no air to his windpipe, I can't make out the words.

"What the hell are you doing here? Where is the other guy? Where is the damn money you stole from my trunk?"

I ease up on the pressure a little, and he heaves a breath. "Bobby has it. He went back to Hays last night."

"Then why the hell are you here with a rental car? You better start making sense right now, if you want to live out the day."

He doesn't answer, so I press my forearm against his throat again. His eyebrows climb as his face reddens. He acts tough at first, but as his chest tries unsuccessfully to hitch a breath, his eyes implore me. His lips jiggle as he's trying to speak.

After a moment, I relax the pressure.

"I'm going to see my cousin in Tulsa," he says, coughing. "Stopped in Stillwater to pick up some pot. That's all."

I slip a hand into each of his front pockets. Find exactly what I'm looking for, which is a folding knife. I flick the blade open and point it at his heart. "Where is my money?"

"I told you. Bobby has it."

I reach around him and snag his wallet. Open it up, and he has only about ten bucks in cash. I take the cash, shove it in my pocket, and then drop the wallet on the ground. Flick my head back toward the front of the diner. "Let's go."

He raises his hands. "What are you talking about?"

"You're going to show me every nook and cranny of your rental car until I believe you don't have my money. And put your damn hands down."

He complies and mopes toward the front. Head down, always clicking his eyes back to me. I stay within a few inches so I can use his body to shield the knife from anyone who might be looking. It's early, but people might notice the knife-wielding man in the parking lot.

For the next five minutes, the redneck explores everything inside the car. He opens the trunk, the glove box, the seat-back pockets.

"I don't have it, see?" he says as he lifts the spare tire in the trunk to show me underneath it.

I consider making him remove the doors or cut the seat cushions, but by now, I do believe this redneck thief. My money isn't here, which is bad news for me. How bad,

I'm not even sure yet. I haven't had time to consider all the implications.

He stands by the door. I'm next to him, with the knife under my shirt.

"I'm sorry, man, this was all Bobby's idea. After what happened at the saloon, he went crazy."

My teeth grind, but even more than anger, I'm feeling the crushing blow of defeat. My simple plan to roll in here and get the shoebox home in two days has gone to hell.

The redneck holds his car keys in his hand.

I can force him to call this Bobby guy and return my money, but when Bobby shows up, he'll likely pull his gun, and someone will end up dead.

I wave toward the car. "Fine. Go."

He glances at my hand, the one concealing the knife. He wants it back. I stand firm until he gets the message that it's mine now, and then he sighs as he enters his rental car.

And as he drives away, I'm standing in the parking lot of Shortcakes, stranded in this God-forsaken town.

CHAPTER THIRTEEN

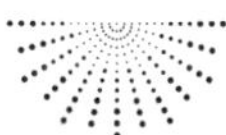

OKLAHOMA - NOW

The bartender refills my cup with one hand as he takes away the empty plate of cheese fries with the other. With the amount of cash left in my wallet, I can have about two more cups before I'm broke. Two more won't get the job done, but it's better than nothing.

I have no way to return to Denver. I have two credit cards in my wallet, and they're both maxed. Even if I could, I wouldn't want to throw down digital money to board a plane, a train, or a bus. If my name shows up on any of those lists, and Gavin will know I'm not in Colorado. That's more damning than him finding out about my impounded car.

After Shortcakes, I even tried my hand at hitchhiking, but a cop car drove by and flashed its lights at me. Maybe hitchhiking is illegal in Oklahoma. I wouldn't know, I've never had to do it before.

I should have forced the redneck thief to drive me back. Didn't even occur to me at that moment.

I could call my boss Frank since he's the only friend I have in the world. But, I can't tell him the truth, and I don't want to lie to the old man. He seems like a decent guy. Calls me "kid" all the time.

"I'm so screwed," I say to the Eskimo Joe's cup in front of me. I sip the watered-down beer and wipe my hands on a napkin.

Around me, it's a lunchtime Tuesday at Joe's. Music pumps from downstairs, and people eat burgers and sip beers. Light from the skylight above shines across the wooden bar in front of me.

I'm out of options, and I have no idea where to go next.

With nothing to do, I heft the shoe box from the seat next to me and set it on the bar. Lift the lid and look inside for the first time in about a year and a half. Since right after the chaos happened in Oklahoma City, but before the feds whisked me away to a safe house to await trial.

A wash of nostalgia settles over me. A photo of me, my sister and brother, and our parents at the Alamo in San Antonio, one of the last happy times before my drinking took hold and ruined every family trip after that one.

And below the family photo, at the top of the pile of letters and other bits of memorabilia is a picture of my best friend and me. A man whose name I've now sworn I'll never say again. Not because I'm angry at him or don't want to remember him. I can't say his name because it makes me see his face in my mind. And that's a blade twisting in my chest.

But looking at these pictures is painful enough.

The photo shows us in Canyonlands National Park, at our campsite the first day. Chester Park? Cheston Park? I can't remember the exact name of the place. It was a wide-open field in the middle of a vast array of rock spires. My friend has his arm around me, grinning his devilish grin. I'm exhausted, not used to hiking long distances. I remember that moment, burned in time on this photo, printed only a few days before his death. A couple minutes after it was taken, we found Travis Pyuen's campsite, then he descended from a hidden spot in the rocks above us and kicked both of our asses. Easily.

We had no idea what we were up against. But we would soon find out.

"Rough day?" the bartender says, leaning against the other side of the bar. There's a white towel resting on his shoulder, the end of it dangling in the air.

"You could say that."

He nods, pushing out his lower lip. Very empathetic. "I hear you. What's the deal?"

"I wanted something really bad, and I was willing to do anything to get it. And now, I've got it, but I didn't think it through, and all those little details I should have considered have come back to bite me in the ass."

He pushes out his lower lip, standing up to his full height. "I hear you. I've been trying to teach my dog how to fetch me beers from my fridge, right? He's great at it, up until the part where he has to close the fridge door. He gets so excited, he slams it shut with his paws, and it breaks half the stuff inside. Ketchup and milk and shit everywhere."

"That's rough."

"Yeah, it is." His head turns toward someone at the other end of the bar, wagging a finger in the air. The bartender taps the bar a couple times in front of me to seal our conversation, then he walks off to aid this other customer. At least he didn't ask me about the shoebox.

I sigh, my friend's smiling face in the photo boring into my heart.

If I knew he would be dead within a few years, would I have done things differently? Hard to say. All I understood then, on that day, was that we were in the park on a specific mission that turned out to differ completely from what we had expected.

We barely made it out alive.

Someone enters my field of vision from the left, so I scoop up the photos and drop them back in the box. Tilt my head to see two people standing at the bar next to me. One, a woman, slim but somehow curvy, and a man, hairy and large, oversized limbs like a cartoon character.

The woman smiles at me as they're waiting for the bartender. Her smile lights up her face in a way I didn't anticipate. She has green eyes like emeralds and red hair, a deep auburn. Almost brown, but with enough tint you can't call her a brunette. Her skin is pale and smooth. She stands out like a rose in a field of lilies, and I'm caught off guard by her beauty. I can only stare.

The man next to her smiles as well, and he's equally breathtaking. Not handsome, but more like a force to be reckoned with. He's at least 6'4", with bushy hair pulled back into a frizzy ponytail and a beard that extends his already-wide face two inches in each direction. He may be the hairiest person I've ever seen.

My friend used to call these sorts of people *wookies*.

The bartender is at the other end of the bar, still helping someone else. When they notice this, they both turn to me. The wookie speaks first. His smile is so big it turns his face into a wince. "Howdy."

"Hello."

He extends a meaty hand. "I'm Poppa Bear." His voice is deep and throaty. Carries a lot of weight.

"Poppa Bear?"

Now I notice he's wearing a wedding band, and so is she. They're a couple.

His smile turns into a chuckle, the sort of thing to make his belly jiggle. And as for bellies, his is another force to be reckoned with.

"Well, that's my name, so that's what you should call me."

I roll my fingers across the bar. "Oh, okay."

"They call him Poppa Bear," the wife says, "but his name is Barry. It's convenient."

I shake Poppa Bear's hand as the woman says, "I'm Cassidy."

My mouth almost forms the word *Michael,* but I catch myself at the last second. Looking at these pictures has placed me squarely in the past.

"Micah."

"Howdy, Micah," Poppa Bear says. "You a local?"

I can tell by the question he is not. The bartender arrives, and Cassidy orders beers for them both. When the beers arrive in the signature large plastic Joe's cups, they both stare at them, musing. Obviously, they've never been here before.

"I'm not local," I say. "Just passing through."

"What brings you here?" Cassidy asks.

I consider this question for a moment, and I'm not even sure anymore. "I'm on a mission to retrieve something important. Well, I was, but now I'm stranded here."

Cassidy frowns, and somehow, she still looks gorgeous doing it. "That's too bad. Did you retrieve the thing?"

"I did."

"And where were you headed after that?"

"Denver."

Her eyes shoot wide, and she tugs on Poppa Bear's shirt.

Poppa Bear maintains a flat expression. "You don't say, brother."

"I do say."

"Excuse us a second," she says, then she pulls him over toward a table. They have an animated chat that lasts for thirty seconds. She's waving her hands, leaning into her argument, and he's slowly shaking his head. Back and forth, she's trying to convince him, and he slowly warms to the idea. I can't read lips, but I don't have to.

After another minute, he finally relents, and they return to me. She's beaming.

"We're in from Birmingham," Poppa Bear says, "on our way to Fairview to pick up a couple friends of ours." He leans closer, like he's about to drop a knowledge-bomb on me. "And then, we're headed west, and then up to Denver. Seems like the gods have put you right in our path."

When Cassidy tugged on his shirt, I had a feeling the conversation was headed in this direction. But then, when he mentioned picking up his friends, my heart sank.

"Oh," I say, "if you're picking up some friends, probably going to be crowded in your back seat."

Poppa Bear chuckles. "Plenty of room, brother. More room than we know what to do with, to be honest with you. If you'd like to catch a ride with us, you're absolutely welcome to join."

CHAPTER FOURTEEN

UTAH - FOUR YEARS AGO

For the first ten minutes or so after Travis descended from the rocks and kicked our asses, Pug and I said nothing. There wasn't anything to say. He'd knocked us out and slipped away unseen. We were left to sit, alone, to lick our wounds and dissect how it had all happened so fast, so surprisingly, so completely.

And then, we puzzled over how he'd slipped away during the few seconds Pug and I were both knocked out. Why he'd only taken some of his things with him when he'd fled.

We felt like idiots. Clearly, we had no idea who we were dealing with here. And we had no route to chase after him. We debated setting off to search for him, but agreed we didn't want to be stuck away from our campsite in fading light. Plus, Pug was sore from the fight, and I really wanted to stay in one spot and get drunk.

So, as the afternoon faded, Pug and I set up our camp, in the same spot Travis had used. Figured we might as well.

As Pug assembled the camp stove and got to work cooking our meal-in-a-bag meat and pasta dinner, I uncapped the first of the three bottles of bourbon. Had been thinking about a drink all day, but I knew it would have been hell trying to hike after slugging back enough of the bottle to make me feel better.

I stared up above us as the stars came into focus. In the sky appeared Orion, that arrangement of fat and bright stars I could always isolate from the rest. Along with the severed head of Boba Fett I carried with me, Orion was my other confidant. Not as much as Boba was, but we did chat from time to time.

Pug lifted the pot of boiling water and then poured it into the bag. He set a timer on his phone, then he leaned back and stared at me. Quiet tension on his face. "I have to tell you something."

"Okay."

He leaned forward, pressing his hands together. Hard. Then, he jumped up and paced around, hands on his hips. Grimacing with each step. He was wearing flip-flops, having shed the heavy duty hiking boots while we set up camp. His sandals shuffled through the sand around our campsite.

"What is it, Pug?"

He dropped to a knee and picked up a small rock from

the ground. Flat, like the sort you'd skip across a lake. He turned it over in his hands, letting his fingers caress the surface. "I don't know. I don't want to tell you this, but I have to."

This whole thing was starting to creep me out. "Well, okay then. Let's hear it."

Again, he paused. I could tell he was stalling.

Finally, after a few more false starts, he said, "does it bother you that we don't know what Gus does for a living?"

"What do you mean?"

"Do you ever look inside those packages he asks you to deliver?"

I shook my head. "I try not to think about it."

"You're okay with that?"

"I don't know. What do you want me to say? I know what's inside those packages isn't life-saving medications for orphans. I know whatever Gus and everyone else is doing isn't legal. But the money is good, and it's not like we have anything better going on right now. I'm not sure who would even hire me."

Pug nodded as he hovered over the boil-in-a-bag dinner, still cooking itself. He shifted the bag back and forth, mixing the contents.

"What do you think would happen if we decided to quit working for Gus?"

I shrugged. "No idea. But why would we? It's good money. Great money."

"Yeah. That's true."

"Where's all this coming from?" I asked.

"The other day, I went along with Gus' new guy, Ramón? Have you met him?"

I nodded. Had encountered him once and wasn't impressed. He would supposedly become a management layer between guys like Gus and guys like Pug and me. Gus was traveling more frequently, so he wanted someone based in OKC to manage us.

"Yeah, I met him. Seems like a prick. Showy guy, trying to prove something. Probably into coke and ecstasy and all that other stuff. Why do you ask?"

"Me and him and Gus went out to see some guy Gus had loaned money to. He owns a little shit-kicker bar in Crescent. Anyway, the guy couldn't pay back the loan, so Gus and Ramón beat the crap out of him. Knocked him around, slammed his head down on the bar. I watched the guy spit teeth onto the floor. This was in the middle of the day, and there were other people in his bar. Paying customers."

A chill ran down my spine. "That's brutal."

"And then, after, Gus took us out for tacos. Never mentioned a word of it, even as he excused himself to go to the bathroom to wash a spot of blood off his shirt."

"Maybe the bar owner deserved it," I said.

He eyed me. "You believe that?"

I shook my head.

Pug squeezed the dinner bag a few times and checked

the timer on his phone. He set the bag on the ground and shifted onto a nearby rock. Leaned forward, head down, elbows on knees and hands clasped. Judging by his constant fidgeting, he was more troubled by this than he let on.

"Is this all you wanted to tell me?" I said.

He flexed his hands a few times, then shook them out. "Well, I guess I shouldn't put it off any longer."

"What?" I said as I studied the bottle of bourbon. It was half gone, and I had a nice buzz sloshing back and forth inside my brain. Didn't feel the aches and pains from the day anymore.

"I had a difficult conversation with my parents the other day. And now, I need to have a difficult conversation with you, too."

"Pug, what are you talking about?"

His eyes tracked all around us, at the sinking sun and the rock spires. "And what a terrible place for me to do this. Out here, in the middle of nowhere."

"You're scaring me."

He lifted his head, and I could see the fear written in his eyes. I had a flash of panic that he was about to tell me he had cancer or AIDS or that he had to move to South America.

Pug opened his mouth to speak, then paused and snatched his pack of smokes. He withdrew two and held one out to me, but I waved it off. I rarely smoked. Only when drunk enough to make a bad decision like that, and I was not nearly drunk enough.

"Tell me what's going on," I said. Felt my shoulders tensing. "Just spit it out."

He looked into my eyes. His knee bounced up and down, making his body vibrate. My heart beat so fast, I started to see spots at the edge of my vision.

"I have to tell you something. After I saw what Gus did the other day to that guy, I was thinking about what would happen to you if something ever happened to me."

"Please don't speak in riddles."

He grimaced. "I'm saying how you wouldn't ever have known me. The real me."

"Okay, shit, Pug, just get to it. Dying here."

"I'm... I'm gay."

I let all the air whoosh out of my lungs and rolled my shoulders a few times. Emitted a chirp of a laugh.

"Seriously?" I said. "That's your big news you've got me all panicked about?"

He sat up a little straighter, his brow creased. "I don't understand. This is the biggest thing I've ever told anyone in my entire life. Why are you laughing?"

"I mean, *obviously* you're gay, Phillip Gillespie. I've known since we were in school."

"You... you have?"

I sipped the bottle, nodded, and then handed it to him. He held it out, his eyes tracking mine for a few seconds. Then, he chuckled as he took a swig.

"I've been nervous all day about telling you," he said. "I

thought I was going to poop my pants when we stopped for our mid-morning snack."

"Well, that was dumb."

He stared at the bottle and then passed it back to me. "Yeah, I guess it was. Maybe I knew you knew. But I've never said it out loud."

"Now that you did it, do you feel better?"

He nodded. "I guess. Telling my parents was rough. They weren't happy, but what are they going to do? I'm an adult, with my own job and my own money."

"I'm bummed you didn't feel like you could tell me about coming out to your parents."

He looked at me, pain on his face. I'd made him feel guilty about it, which hadn't been my intention.

"No, wait," I said. "That's not what I meant."

"I know," he said, digging his foot around in the sand. "With all this going on out here, with this Travis guy, I don't know about anything anymore."

"Don't you think Travis is probably long gone?"

He hesitated for a few moments, mulling his words. "Maybe. Maybe not. But I think we owe it to Gus to spend tomorrow looking for him before we call it and head back."

"That works for me. He's owed an ass-whooping for what he did to us."

Pug looked at the Springfield 1911 sitting on the ground next to me, loaded and ready to go. Then, the timer on Pug's phone dinged. Dinner was ready.

PAPER TIGER

CHAPTER FIFTEEN

OKLAHOMA - NOW

The RV rolls along Highway 51. Poppa Bear is up front, driving. His chair is like something I'd expect to see on a spaceship. Humongous. Cassidy sits in the passenger seat. I'm on the couch, against the wall, behind Poppa Bear. The couch is in the "kitchen" area. Behind that is a table, which I've been told will collapse to make room for cots. When we pick up these two people in Fairview, we'll need every available space for all five of us to sleep.

Beyond the table is the utility area, with a washer and dryer, plus a sink. Then the bathroom section, and the master bedroom with a queen-sized bed. It's like a mobile apartment. Huge inside. I can't understand how Poppa Bear pilots this thing. He doesn't seem to have any trouble, as he and Cassidy are listening to the Grateful Dead and singing along while this massive rectangle with wheels hurdles down the highway.

Sitting behind them, perched on the couch, I feel like a failure. Like a mooch. Yes, I got my shoebox, but I've lost all control now. I'm at the mercy of these people. It does set my mind at ease that they seem cool, but only a little. I don't like feeling indebted and under the thumb of anyone anymore.

I have eleven dollars and a shoebox of memories at my disposal. The shoebox is next to me on the couch because I'm not sure where to put it. Fortunately, my two hosts haven't said a word about it. It probably wouldn't be a big deal. *Here's a picture of me and my friend in Utah, one of us at the Riverwalk in OKC, plus some old love letters and a couple of flash drives.* I doubt they would even care.

But after everything I've been through so far to retrieve this shoebox, I don't want to let it out of my sight. It's the only piece of the past I have left.

Fairview is up near the panhandle of Oklahoma, but I don't think I've ever been there. Oklahoma has so many tiny towns, you can blink and miss a dozen of them as you're driving through. Most of them are so small, the locals identify by the county name instead. You might only know which specific one you're in by glimpsing the lettering on the nearest water tower.

We're on the road for ninety minutes, driving, while my hosts shuffle through a good chunk of The Grateful Dead's catalog. Singing along with every word. I have nothing against the Dead, but it's a little before my time. I wasn't one of those tie-dyed, shaggy-haired, pot-smoking hippies in school. Smoking pot tended to get in the way of the pursuit of alcohol.

Speaking of alcohol, my throat is quite dry at the moment. Those cups of watery beer from Eskimo Joe's are now a distant memory. With only a few bucks in my pocket, I'm at the mercy of my two hosts. It's not a crisis yet, but I sure would like to wet my whistle.

"What do you do for work?" Cassidy says to me, pivoting in her chair.

"I'm a skip tracer."

"You skipped what?" Poppa Bear says, shouting over the music.

Cassidy turns down the volume and then leans around her chair. Big grin on her face making her eyes sparkle. The smile creasing her lips is electric, and I don't know why. "What's a skip tracer?"

"I find people who don't want to be found, basically. Deadbeat dads, people who skip bail. Mostly, I research them on the internet and help my boss find them. He's a bounty hunter and a bail bondsman."

"Whoa," Poppa Bear says. "That's so cool. I'll bet you get to see all kinds of heavy shit when out on your bounty hunter missions."

I don't want to tell them I've only been doing this for a few months, it's rarely cool, and I don't even know what I'm doing at my job yet. My boss Frank has been patient with me. He has to be because I screw up all the time.

I don't want to tell them that, so I lie.

"Sometimes, sure. I've seen crazy stuff. Some things, I can't tell you about. Get a beer or two in me, though, and we'll see if I can't be convinced."

Cassidy eyes me, still beaming. "We just might have to take you up on that offer. The day is young."

Poppa Bear flashes her a look, for only a split second. It's odd. A warning, telling her to break off the conversation. Immediately after, she's turns around, and the music creeps back up to full volume.

For another hour or so, it's back to normal. A soundtrack for a road trip and no conversation. I'm staring out the window at barbed wire fences, red barns, long-abandoned oil wells, cows, horses, pickup trucks, bails of hay spaced out along flat farmland. All the telltale Oklahoma signs of my youth.

Near Fairview, the terrain changes. It becomes hilly, and then I see some bright red mountains in the distance. Not Colorado-sized mountains, but massive enough for Oklahoma. I have no idea where we are, because I've never seen them as tall as this, not even in the hilly part of the state, up in the Northeast area.

Poppa Bear turns the RV off the main road, and we enter *Gloss Mountain State Park*. I only know this because of the sign. Reminds me a bit of the Grand Canyon, with grassy ridges descending into valleys below. Not as big, obviously, but it's still impressive. Red clay dirt provides striking colors everywhere.

"This is Fairview?" I say as I scoot to the forward end of the couch. Only a couple feet behind the driver and passenger chairs.

Poppa Bear turns down the music and says, "nope. But this is where our friends are. We won't be here long. Just going to do a quick sweat and grab our guys. Then we'll be on our way. In and out, bing bang boom."

"Sweat?"

Cassidy grins at me. "Yeah, do you sweat?"

"I mean, I guess, if it's hot out."

She barks a laugh and plays with her hair. "No, that's not what I meant, newbie. You're in for a treat."

Down into a valley, I spot a collection of teepees. It's a little weird that I feel so out of place here because I do have slivers of Native American in my blood. Not much, but my grandfather used to say everyone from Oklahoma has at least some native heritage.

"We're a little late for the ceremony," Poppa Bear says, "but there's still a few people here."

Between the teepees, I see people wearing traditional Native American headdresses and garments, loading gear into the backs of pickup trucks. Coolers, folding chairs, red Solo cups, plastic plates, and silverware. It's like they're breaking down a family reunion.

Aside from the teepees, there are tents and picnic tables. Not much else in this valley of red dirt.

"What is this place?" I say. "What were they doing here?"

"Sun dance ceremony," Cassidy says. "You ever been to one?"

"I don't even know what that is."

She points to an open space, ringed by a wooden fence, with a tall tree in the middle. "That's the warrior tree. I think that's what they call it. The ceremony usually happens in July, but it got moved up, for some reason."

My mind is like a puddle. I have no idea what's going on here.

Poppa Bear guides the RV into a spot next to a tent, and two men stop what they're doing and watch it roll in. They're holding bags in their hands, half-stuffed with sleeping bags and clothes.

Poppa Bear turns to me and says, "it's time to meet Dichali and Ash. Our friends have been waiting here for us."

"Um, okay."

Poppa Bear grins at my confusion and opens the side door. We all three emerge from the RV to find the sun plummeting in the afternoon light. The two men in front of us are brown-skinned, Native American. One with long, braided hair, the other with shorter hair and tattoos ringing his neck.

"Micah," Cassidy says as she points to the tattooed one, "this is Dichali." Then, to the long hair, "this is Ashkii, but you can call him Ash. They're going to travel to Denver with us."

Dichali and Ash stare at me, making no move to shake my hand, or nod a greeting, or do anything at all to acknowledge my presence. After a round of shaking hands with Poppa Bear and Cassidy, they return to breaking down the tent.

Ash pulls a bag from inside the tent, half-unzipped. I can't help but look. There's a sawed-off shotgun inside the bag, barrel poking out.

CHAPTER SIXTEEN

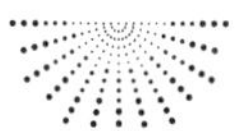

OKLAHOMA - NOW

Despite what Poppa Bear said about us getting on the road right away, we linger at the campsite for quite some time. Dichali and Poppa Bear wander off for an hour, and I'm left to sit in lawn chairs beside the RV with Cassidy and Ash, who crack open a bottle of whiskey and pass it back and forth. When I see it, a wave of relief passes over me. Wasn't sure where I would be able to get a drink today. And, I thought it might seem rude if I rooted around in the cabinets inside the RV since I barely know these people.

Ash and Cassidy make small talk about the sun dance festival for a while. I mostly stare at my phone, but I take my turn whenever the bottle comes around. It's Old Crow, and it burns my throat like swallowing fire, but I don't complain. Even the pain feels good when my throat is this dry.

By the time the sun turns red and Poppa Bear returns, I'm good and drunk. Feeling a little better. However long they've been gone, I'm not sure. Between me, Ash, and Cassidy, maybe five hundred words total have been uttered. But it's been nice to watch the sun sink toward these bright red mountains, to sit quietly, not to worry about things for once.

Of course, I'm thinking about the shotgun I saw in the new guy Ash's bag, but I don't know if I need to *worry* about it, per se.

"Let's go, brother," Poppa Bear says to me upon his return, and I head toward the RV.

"Not that way," Cassidy says. "We need to do a sweat first."

They've mentioned this a few times, and I still don't understand what they're talking about.

She beckons me toward the valley, where a cluster of teepees sit. I'm starting to get a little anxious because I expected us to be on the road by now. But that's only my paranoia talking. Still have four days until Gavin's arrival in Denver, and it's only about a twelve-hour drive from here. Everything is fine.

Poppa Bear lifts up the flap on a teepee, and I'm met with a blast of heat. Inside, there is a rock pit in the middle, with a collection of black rocks next to it, some of them glowing.

"What is this?" I ask.

Tattooed Dichali puts a hand on my arm and guides me

forward, into the teepee. "This is the next step on your journey, Micah."

I step inside, ducking my head. Feel like I'm about to be forced to take an oath and sacrifice a goat. I sure hope not.

Poppa Bear, Ash, Cassidy, and Dichali all take seats around the edge, and now I notice another man, sitting next to the glowing rocks. A pail of water and a ladle next to him. He's an older man, with long braided pigtails, a plain brown shirt, and a pair of Oakley prescription glasses.

"Welcome," he says to me, his face an eerie red glowing from the light of the rocks. "Please, have a seat."

I grab a spot between Cassidy and Dichali, next to the edge of the teepee. If something goes wrong, I'm only two feet from the exit. But why would anything go wrong?

I can't seem to calm down.

The flap closes, and we're now in darkness. The older man begins to chant, and I hear the ladle dip into the water.

Splash. Steam rises in the air, and I'm soaked in an instant. The heat gets into my lungs, and I can barely breathe. Next to me, Dichali removes his shirt and inhales the steam mushrooming below his face. His hands waft it toward his nose as his shoulders rise with each inhalation.

The old man ladles more water onto the rocks, chants louder. The steam is so thick, I can feel it collecting on my forehead and then rushing into my eyes. My body feels heavy, then light, then like my skin is on fire.

This happens over and over again as the old man chants. Time begins to slip as I focus on breathing and trying to ignore the pain of the heat. It's intense. Hard to breathe. My throat closes. Then, somehow, air seeps in. I can't explain it other than to say the sensations gripping my body feel totally out of my control.

I have no idea how long the whole event lasts. Feels like minutes, or hours, or maybe days. Every time the water splashes, heat rushes at me. Sweat continuously cascades down my flesh. My hair is matted to my forehead.

But something strange happens. After a time, I don't feel the heat any longer. Each breath, labored at first, begins to come naturally. My heart rate feels slow, like a deliberate pump of blood with each breath.

I've never experienced anything like it. I'm calm in a way that has never felt possible before.

The old man stops chanting, and then a few seconds pass in silence. "Thank you," he says, and then folds back the flap of the teepee.

A flood of cold air rushes in. I'm startled at the sensation. I feel like all I've known for days has been heat. It's become comfortable. This new sensation of cold is like being tossed naked into a wintry lake, except without the nasty surprise element. My skin feels *radiant.*

I open my eyes and look outside to uncover darkness. Stars winking in the sky above.

Everyone inside the teepee begins to file out, and a

young girl is standing outside, distributing towels. I shiver in the cold air until she hands me one, and I wrap it around my torso. My clothes are slick and clingy.

The strangest sensation courses through my body. I don't know how to describe it. One thing I know for sure, I was well on my way to drunk when I entered, and now I feel stone cold sober. Like all of the alcohol has been deleted from my system. Not even hungover.

"What did you think?" Cassidy says, facing me. She's wearing a flower shirt and a billowing skirt, both items damp and stuck to her skin.

"I don't… I don't know what to say."

Grinning, she reaches up to my face and wipes sweat from my brow. "It's magical, isn't it? Like being born again, but without all the Christian guilt?"

I feel light, made of feathers. "Yeah. I guess it does."

Ash says something to Poppa Bear, and Poppa Bear joins Cassidy and me. "I need to go talk with our friends for a little bit. We'll meet you back at the RV in about two hours, okay? Cass, can you keep our new friend here from walking off the edge of a cliff? I know you're probably feeling a little loopy."

I say nothing. Too dazed. Cassidy agrees to Poppa Bear's request as he, Dichali, and Ash wander off. She's running the towel through her hair.

"Walk with me," she says. "It'll make you feel normal if you get some blood flowing again."

I re-cinch the towel around my waist, and she gestures

toward the lower part of the valley, where the groups of teepees stand out under the moonlight. Like little pyramids, traveling along this spaceship earth.

As we stroll, she laces her fingers through mine. It's a strange feeling, being touched by someone. Every part of my body is hypersensitive right now. Her skin is warm, and it makes mine feel alight with fire. Unreal.

"My first sweat was with a shaman from the Pawnee tribe when I was sixteen," she says. "Now, I need one at least once a week, or I start to feel disconnected. It's like crack or something."

She takes a hearty breath, her shoulders rising. I note how her shirt, slick with sweat, curves around her breasts. I'm trying not to stare, but I can't help myself.

"Jasper the cat belongs to everyone," I say, but I don't know why.

"Huh?"

"Nothing. I've never done this before. A sweat."

She giggles. "Obviously not. You look like a kid in the candy store. I don't think you've closed your mouth since you walked out of there."

She's right. I close my mouth.

We stop in front of a teepee, and she screws her face up to stare at the sky. "Look. Full moon."

I look up, and it's not quite a full moon, but it's close. She tilts her head back and sucks in a breath, then she lets out a sound like a muted howl. A wolf imitation. I'm taken back at first, then after a few seconds of this, find myself smiling and giggling at the craziness of it.

She pokes me in the ribs. "Come on. Howl with me." And she resumes howling at the cheese moon above us.

I don't know what comes over me, but I find myself doing it, too. Both of us, mouths pointed skyward, letting our animal sides unleash at the heavens.

She takes a step toward me and slides a hand around my waist. When I pull back, she moves with me. Like we're dancing.

"This is okay," she says. "I want this."

Then she's up on her tiptoes to kiss me, and when her lips touch mine, I feel like I've been zapped with a laser beam. Like a million dollars' worth of fireworks are exploding inside my head, all at once.

She opens the flap on the teepee and ushers me inside. Within two seconds, she's lifting up her shirt. It's dark, and I can only make out shadows. Her fingers remove my shirt and unwrap the towel from around my waist.

She guides my hands to her hips, and then I'm pushing down her skirt. I know this tryst is a bad idea, but I can't help myself. My brain is pounding, firing sensations at a thousand miles per hour. Desire is quicksand, and I'm barely keeping my head above the surface.

This is wrong. I shouldn't do this. She's a married woman, and I'm about to do something I won't be able to undo.

But it's as if I'm not in control of my own limbs as my fingers glide over her flesh.

When I run my hands back up her thighs, I feel scars on her hips. My eyes drift down to see what look like knife slashes, or maybe whip marks.

She notices me noticing.

"What's that?" I say.

A frown darkens her face. "Some people aren't as nice as you think they are."

"Poppa Bear?"

She eases closer and unbuttons my jeans. "I don't want to talk about him. I don't want to talk at all."

CHAPTER SEVENTEEN

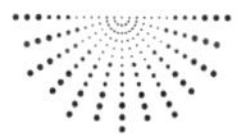

UTAH - FOUR YEARS AGO

Pug and I crossed Chesler Park as the sun rose in the east. A stark blue sky materialized above me. Huge, clear, clean. I'd never seen anything like it before. Like the entirety of the ocean above us, hanging in space.

Once, in high school, Pug and I and a few of our friends got smashed on cheap wine and went to a planetarium laser light show. While we'd done the whole thing ironically, I had to admit the pinholes of light in the blackness above filled me with wonder. There was something about the sky, about the vastness of it. Sometimes, it could make me feel small. Sometimes, though, it could make me believe anything was possible.

This morning, I was mostly feeling my teeth clattering. I'd wrapped myself in every layer available because April in Utah was apparently quite a bit colder than April in Oklahoma. Nobody told me.

Chesler Park was a wide open expanse of flat grassland. A few city blocks wide, ringed by walls made up of pale rock spires colored with beige, yellow, and an earthy pale pink. Big enough that you had to squint to detect detail on the faraway spires. A crisscrossing web of dirt trails leading to various edges of the park sliced the grasslands, turning them into segments. I trailed Pug as he followed one of those skinny paths through the grass, hungover, my shoulders aching.

I'd finished one of my three bottles of bourbon the night before. Two left. I wasn't sure how long we'd be out here, but it was something to keep in mind. Surely no more than one additional day.

As long as we accomplished our task, which would make the boss happy, this whole venture wouldn't take long.

But, I'd been thinking that morning about what Pug had told me about our boss Gus so violently assaulting a man. And that I had no idea what he did for a living, and therefore, what I did for a living.

Not fun things to think about. Too easy to let my brain sink into a spiral of doubt and confusion.

As we neared one wall of the park, the rock spires came into focus. I could see it wasn't a solid wall of rock, but many individual spires with passageways between them. Some large, some little cracks in the rock.

"You know where you're going?" I said.

He held up the park map, and then pursed his lips. "If he's still here, good chance we'll find him in one of these slot canyons along the side."

"Do you think he's still here?"

"Not if he's smart. We've got his backcountry permit and half his gear, so he should've gotten the hell out of here."

I sipped my water bottle and eyed Pug. "Yeah, but do you *think* he's still here?"

Pug mused on this for a moment. "I do. I can't say why, but I think he's still around. Maybe he expects he's going to hunt us, to get us off the trail."

"Or, maybe Travis *is* smart, and he bailed after our fight yesterday."

He shrugged. "Could be."

"Worst-case, we can tell Gus we did all we could."

But, I wondered if that was the actual worst case. Gustavo Salazar had been good to me, but I'd never seen his violent side. If this Travis guy had stolen from him and roughed up Gus' wife, how angry would he be with us for letting him go with no consequences?

Pug headed for an opening between two large spires leaning together like an inverse letter *V*. A dark slit in the rock, only a few feet wide and ten feet tall. At the lip of the opening, Pug paused to light a cigarette.

"Do you want to talk about Gus and—"

"No," he said. "I don't."

"Okay then."

His face softened. "Sorry, Mikey. I didn't mean it like that. Just got too much on my mind right now."

"No, I get why you don't want to. No trouble." I flicked my head toward the opening in the rock. "What's the plan in there?"

"I'm not sure. Looking for something to point us in the right direction. I'm hoping we can run into some other backpackers who'll have seen this Asian bodybuilder with the Fists-Of-Fury and can tell us where he's holed up."

"That's a long shot. I haven't seen another person since yesterday afternoon."

He nodded. "True. But it's the best we have right now."

I dropped to a knee and put both hands over my heart. "Your best is good enough for me, dear Pugsley."

He smirked, then leaned over and socked me on the shoulder. A good one, too. Hurt like hell.

"Just 'cuz you know I'm gay doesn't mean I won't still kick your ass."

I stood, rubbing my shoulder. "I would expect nothing less." Then, I pointed into the darkness. "Lead on, trail guide."

We ventured into the crack, with our pistols and our water bottles and little else. On the other side of the dark divide, I found a dirt path snaking between cliff walls a hundred feet high. The vastness of it startled me, especially since the canyon was only about twenty feet wide. Like being in the bottom of a dream.

"Holy shit," I said.

"That's one way to describe it."

Pug pointed at a drop-off in the path, sixty feet ahead. We approached cautiously to find a small cliff at the edge of the path, leading down to a lower-level slot canyon below. Maybe twenty feet. But, when I leaned forward, I noted someone had angled a log against the cliff wall. It reached almost to the top. The log had notches cut into it every few feet, made into a ladder.

"That's convenient," I said. "Someone put a lot of work into that thing."

Pug hooked his water bottle's carabiner onto his belt loop and then turned around. He took a step down, onto the log ladder. And then another.

"Feel sturdy?"

He nodded as his head disappeared below the edge of the cliff. "It's all good. No problems here."

I followed him down once he'd made it to the ground, and was on the lower level with him in ten seconds. Somehow, it felt a few degrees cooler.

I gazed back at the log ladder. Worried it might crumble, because it looked like it had been here a few years. Probably thousands of people had used that thing to climb in and out of this little sub-canyon.

We headed to the path deeper into the canyon to find it ended in a thousand feet at a flat wall. Sheer, slick, and no way to scale the surface. But along the way, we'd seen a couple of side-facing slot canyons, so we turned back toward them. One on the right, and one on the left. The right-facing one also ended after two hundred feet in. Just a sandy path marked by the same sheer walls and a dead end.

We traced our steps back out to the main canyon and ventured toward the other slot. And what we found there was so strange, I felt like I'd been transported into a horror movie. Both of us paused at the lip of the slot for a few seconds before entering.

This slot canyon was more like a cave, as the walls were mostly closed at the top and there was no way out on the far side. Only little slivers of light trickled through. But what was on the ground was far more interesting. Cairns, the little deliberate piles of rocks normally used to mark trails, were everywhere. Literally hundreds of them, all over the floor of this stretch of the canyon. Some were stacked near the walls, like decorations.

"What the hell is this?" I said.

"Like a horror movie."

"I was just thinking that same thing."

Pug pointed at his forehead and then at mine. Grinned. We shared a brain, apparently.

"Who do you think put all these cairns in here?" I said. "This must have taken someone weeks to do all this."

He shrugged and then turned his ear back toward the entrance. "Do you hear that?"

"No, what?"

"It's like a crackling."

I stilled my breathing and closed my eyes, and I could hear it, too. Crackling, snapping, sizzling.

Like a campfire.

We both spun and ran toward the slot entrance, back to the main canyon. And, at the cliff where we'd descended, Travis Pyuen was standing at the top with a box of lighter fluid in his hand. Below him, the ladder-log was in flames. But you could hardly call it a log anymore. The thing was a stick of fire, sending reddened bits of ember thirty feet into the sky.

It crumbled and then snapped in half as trails of black and red floated up toward Travis. I noted the look on his face. Half-grin, half-sneer.

I whipped out my pistol and closed one eye to aim down the sight, but Travis disappeared back into the canyon before I could get my finger over the trigger.

Pug rushed forward toward the log. By now, the whole thing was engulfed in flames, and it broke again and then collapsed into a fiery puddle at the bottom of the canyon. The flames quickly slowed and died, leaving black marks along the now-unclimbable cliff wall.

Our ladder out had been destroyed. We were trapped down here.

CHAPTER EIGHTEEN

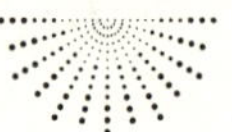

OKLAHOMA - NOW

A half hour later, we're in the RV, our sweat-drenched clothes in the washer. She's changed, and I'm wearing a giant pair of sweatpants and a shirt that belong to Poppa Bear. We're passing a bottle of Old Crow back and forth, and after two sips, I'm tipsy. I still don't understand what that sweat lodge episode has done to me. If this can reduce my alcohol tolerance to nil on a regular basis, imagine how much that could cut into my liquor budget.

I'm on the couch, feeling the warmth of the whiskey and the afterglow of sex. She's in the kitchen, slathering red sauce and cheese on bagels. She pops them in the toaster oven and then winks at me from the kitchen. I can't get over the light in her eyes, the way her skin reminds me of milk.

I want to ask her if she feels guilty about what we've

done. It's not right. We did a bad thing. But, I can't even make the words form on my lips. Too drunk. I'm not capable of having a reasonable conversation right now.

When she closes the toaster oven door, she leans against the counter, grinning at me. "I have fun with you."

"Thanks. I have fun with you, too."

I hold the bottle of Old Crow out to her, and she slinks around the counter to snag it from me. Her fingers brush up against mine, and I can feel the fire race up my arm, down my torso, straight to my crotch.

"But I need to tell you something," she says. "What you saw back there, in the valley. What I said about Poppa Bear..."

"It's none of my business," I say.

A few seconds pass before she answers. "No, it's not. But you saw what you saw, and I said what I said. It's true, but I don't want you to think he's a monster. He gets a little angry sometimes, but who doesn't, you know? There's a lot going on in the world right now to be angry about."

I look at the bottle of Old Crow in my hands. It's mostly gone, and I'm hammered. Part of me wants to grab Cassidy by the shoulders and tell her she's brainwashed. Tell her Poppa Bear *is* a monster, and he's never going to change. But the other part of me knows telling her will do no good. I'm sure she's heard it before.

And, I don't even know for a fact he's the one who gave her those scars. She didn't confirm it. Plus, although I recently had sex with her, I don't know Cassidy at all. Maybe I shouldn't believe a word she says.

The point is, I don't know anything about anything, and I'm sure Boba Fett would agree with me.

So instead, I say nothing and sit with her on the couch. I don't want to leave her side. My drunken brain tells me to be here with her, holding her, making sure she understands she is safe with me. I can do that much, at least.

"Ash and Dichali," I say. "Friends of yours?"

"Yeah, we've known them for a long time. I know they look like a couple of stand-offish jerks, but they're all bark. Trust me."

A wave of nausea overcomes me, so I excuse myself to use the bathroom. I can't avoid bumping into everything between the couch and the toilet. My head swims in the most pleasant way. My body feels light and heavy, impervious to pain. I could take a baseball bat to the stomach, and I doubt I would even flinch.

In the bathroom, when I see my doofy reflection in the mirror, I can't help but lapse into a giggling fit. It's unreal to think I got laid only thirty minutes ago. Been a while since the last time. My eyes are bloodshot, my lips are pulled into a grin like a kid on his first venture to a strip club. I'm a mess, and it's cracking me up.

The nausea passes quickly. When I come out of the bathroom, Cassidy holds my shoebox in her lap, thumbing through the pictures. She looks up. "Is this okay?"

"What are you doing?"

"It was just sitting right here. I had to know what was inside it."

Maybe I should feel angry, but I'm drunk and woozy and have no energy to engage in an argument.

She holds up the picture of me and my best friend, in Utah. "Who's this cutie?"

"He was a friend of mine who passed away. My best friend."

Her face falls, and I feel a little guilty. I don't want to imply she's invaded my private space and desecrated my memories of a dead friend. In a way, that is what she's done, but I don't want to feel angry with her. I want this to be no big deal.

"What is all this stuff?" she says, flipping through the pile of letters and in-class notes from high school.

"It's what I came back for."

Her eyebrow cocks. "You drove halfway across the country to get a shoebox?"

"Yes," I say, and I know I should stop there. I should curl up on the couch and go to sleep. But I don't. Before I know what's happening, my mouth opens, and the words spill out. Once it starts, I can't stop. "My name isn't Micah. At least, it wasn't always Micah. I was born with a different name. Michael McBriar, although the friend of mine you see in those photos used to call me Mikey.

"About five or six years ago, I got mixed up with some bad people, and I later got arrested. There was a whole thing with a trial and a big lie I had to tell my family, and a lot of that is a blur now. But most of them are in jail, and I live in Colorado, with a new name."

Her mouth is open, her eyes wide. "Whoa. That's unreal."

She opens a drawer next to the couch and removes a tray lined with rolling papers and weed. She breaks up a couple of buds and drops them in the paper, and then rolls and licks the joint. The whole process takes about twenty seconds.

She holds it out to me along with a lighter. I wave her off. I'm pretty sure, as drunk as I am, one hit from a joint will make me barf all over the inside of the RV. "Never really been my thing."

She shrugs and lights it. Takes a deep puff and then stares at the shoebox. "This is who you used to be, isn't it? Memories of a life that doesn't exist anymore."

I nod, and she pats the couch next to her. I sit.

"Whatever your name is, I'm glad you came into my life. I feel like we were supposed to meet. All the shit you've been through to get here boggles my mind."

"I'm glad I met you too," I say, and I can hear how slurred my words are. *Met you* came out as *meh-shoo*.

Maybe telling her my secrets is a terrible idea and will blow up in my face. Right now, though, I can barely string two thoughts together.

Her eyes flick down to my lips, then back to my eyes. As confused as I am, I do know this is my cue to kiss her.

But, before I can, the door to the RV opens.

CHAPTER NINETEEN

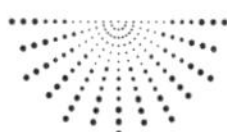

OKLAHOMA - NOW

Poppa Bear, Dichali, and Ash board the RV. Cassidy and I were sitting far enough apart on the couch that no one seems to think anything strange is going on.

I point at the giant sweatpants and make eye contact with Poppa Bear. "Sorry, I didn't have a chance to ask. My clothes are in the washer."

He waves a meaty hand in dismissal. "No worries, brother. What's mine is yours."

I study him for any hint of suspicion. It's at that moment the wave of guilt over what's happened curls around me like a boa constrictor. I slept with a woman who has pledged her life to someone else. Even though it wasn't my idea, and even though she was the one who kept upping the ante, it's not as if I'm blameless. Cassidy wasn't alone in that teepee. I never pushed her off me, or walked away, or voiced any real concern. I let it all happen. I wanted it to happen.

And now I've taken something that doesn't belong to me. If I weren't so drunk at this moment, the guilt might cripple me. But, I'm too numb for that. Later, though, if I allow myself to sober up, the weight of it will probably collapse on me like a toppled Sumo wrestler.

The two newest members of our crew sit in the chairs on opposite sides of the table, but they both turn to stare at me. Cassidy rises from the couch and saunters to the front of the RV.

Ash removes a flask from his pants pocket, hits a big swig, and then passes it to Dichali. Dichali tilts it back and gulps, then he makes a face like he's breathing fire. Ash chuckles at him.

How little they say bothers me. It's intimidating, and maybe that's the point. I saw Nashoba's shotgun. There's a good chance he meant for me to see it. He wants me to keep my distance, so I don't get too curious about their real purpose for heading west.

"You from Denver?" Ash says, eying me. His tone sounds like a friendly conversation-starter when coming out of his mouth, but his face is cold and stoic. Like he's questioning me under the hot lights of a police interrogation room.

"Not originally. I'm from outside Tulsa."

"Then what's in Denver?"

"My destination."

Dichali laughs a little, but Ash doesn't seem to think it's all that funny. He rises from the chair and marches off to the bathroom.

Cassidy is up in the passenger seat, feet up on the dash. She's wearing boxer shorts with no socks and no shoes. Her toes spread out, her knees bent. On the tops of her feet are the faded hints of tan lines from sandals.

She draws on her left thigh with a Sharpie marker. Making intricate little patterns, like a henna tattoo.

"You been in Denver long?" Dichali says, breaking my stare at Cassidy.

"Uh, no. I moved there a few months ago."

Dichali nods and blinks at me. Despite the neck tattoo and the semi-permanent scowl on his face, he doesn't seem as gruff or as menacing as Ash. Which, in some ways, makes Dichali more dangerous. You know a mountain lion will attack you, but a moose will seem harmless. Until it's not.

"I spent some time in Colorado Springs," he says. "Air Force."

"Really?"

He sucks his teeth and closes his eyes, then leans back. I guess the conversation is over now.

Poppa Bear kneels in front of me, holding a map. "Hey, Micah, I think it's a good time to let you know about our itinerary. I know you said this morning you need to be back before the weekend. So, I want you to know what to expect. I don't want you freaking out, thinking we're going to make a dozen more of these sorts of stops between here and the mountains. It's not like that."

"I appreciate the heads up." When I try to focus my eyes on examining the map, the room spins a little. I'm beyond drunk by now and starting to crave a horizontal surface to pass out. My head keeps tilting forward.

He points to a green spot on the map, where we are in Gloss Mountain State Park. His finger drifts west. "We're going to stay off the interstate for a little bit and go up into the panhandle because we need to go see some people out past Guymon tomorrow. After that, we'll hook up with I-25 and head north, up through Colorado Springs. We'll have you home by bedtime tomorrow. Sound good?"

"Sure," I say, swaying in place.

Poppa Bear grins. "You look like you're ready to hit the sack. Why don't you take the bed for a few hours? I think we're going to stay up and do a little maintenance on the RV. We'll get going in a bit, but it's fair game until then. If you want to crash for a couple hours, it's all yours."

"Sure," I say, barely legible. Now, the room is not only spinning, but it's also like I'm somersaulting through it. I don't feel like I'm going to puke, but if I even smell alcohol, it could happen. I wouldn't be surprised.

"We'll come wake you up in a few. That okay?"

"Sure." I struggle to my feet and bumble along the RV. Both Dichali and Ashkii give me odd looks, but I'm too drunk and tired to care anymore. I careen into the bedroom and flop down on the bed.

My eyes slam shut. But then, a moment later, open again. Not quite ready to pass out.

I note something on the edge of the bed. A bag. I reach out to move it away, then I realize this is Ash's bag.

I slump off the bed and shut the door to the bedroom. Takes an immense amount of will to stay upright while accomplishing this monumental task.

Then, I open the bag. My heart stops.

Inside, in addition to the shotgun, are several pistols, a couple pounds of weed, bags of what look like mushrooms, heroin, random pills, and sheet upon sheet of LSD. Bottles of unidentified liquid. A dozen pistol magazines. Three straight razors. A brick of something white, probably cocaine.

And, one other brick. This is the one that sends me into a panic. A brick of something white and heavy, like plastic explosive.

These aren't hippie travelers, cruising to Denver for an outdoor music festival or something benign like that. These are gangsters, with enough material in this bag to start a drug war.

CHAPTER TWENTY

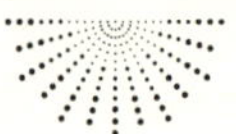

UTAH - FOUR YEARS AGO

In front of us, the ladder made from the carved log burned, now disintegrated into pieces. Smoking and smoldering, the chunks below propagated smoke up along the cliff wall and into the air. I don't know how much lighter fluid Travis dumped on there before he torched it, but it must have been a lot. The thing had turned into kindling in mere seconds. Now it was nothing.

"This is bad," Pug said.

"Yeah."

I approached the still-burning husk of the log to get a closer look at the cliff wall. Rising twenty feet above our heads, there was no way we could shimmy up that surface. The canyon walls on either side were practically sheer, with no foot and hand holds. Maybe if either of us were world-class rock climbers, we could pull it off. But we were flat-landers from Oklahoma. Our state didn't breed too many world-class rock climbers.

"It's too high," Pug said.

"Yeah, it looks that way."

He unclipped his water bottle and held it up. About half full, twelve ounces. When he scrutinized the water level, my heart sank. I knew what he was thinking. I didn't want to look at my own water bottle because I'd have to admit the same fears about being trapped down here.

A moment of panic hit when I realized my bourbon supply was a half mile away, back at the campsite.

"There's got to be another way out," I said.

"Maybe."

I walked a few feet back down the path, looking for another log we could use to rebuild the ladder. There were a few shrubs and one dinky tree jutting up from the desert floor, but the branches were much too thin to support our weight.

"The thing I don't understand," Pug said, "is why he stuck around. I mean, I hoped he would still be here, but I figured it was a long shot."

"Not as far-fetched as it would seem, I guess. But that was definitely him up there, trying to slit our throats with his can of lighter fluid."

Pug put his hands on his hips. "But he knows we're here to take him back to pay for what he did. Why not rush out of here the second he sees us?"

I considered this for a moment. "Because he wants to

make sure we're dead. He doesn't want us reporting back that we saw him and he's still out there."

Pug had no answer for this, but I could see he agreed with me. It was the only explanation. Travis had no choice but to kill us now, and we had no choice but to stop him.

If we could even get out of here.

We shuffled down the barren path toward the crossroads in the slot canyon. Ahead, it dead-ended when the canyons narrowed to a point. To the left, another dead-end canyon. And to the right, the freaky cairn-filled cave. On the initial pass a few minutes ago, none of these places had routes up to the top, which would lead back to Chesler Park. No, this chasm down here contained no visible way out.

I first ventured into the slot canyon across from the cairn lair but stopped quickly. Nothing. The sides of the canyon shot a hundred feet in the air, sometimes ten feet across, sometimes fifty. I could see places up above that might support a hand or a foot, but not enough of them. No way would I trust myself to climb all the way up there. Halfway up, losing a hold, then falling, breaking a leg. We would die here for sure, in that case.

"Not looking good," he said.

"I agree."

"Did you bring your flask with you?"

I shook my head as I dug my fingers into my palms until I could feel the half-moons of my fingernails cutting into my flesh. "It's back at the campsite."

"Really?"

"I know, I know. This would be the perfect time to have it, but I thought we wanted to travel as light as possible during the day."

He drummed his hands against his thighs for a few seconds. "Okay. This is fine. We can't go this way, and now we know that for sure."

I pointed toward the cairn cave. "Let's try this."

"What do you think we'll find? I can see the dead-end from here."

Then I did examine my water bottle and found it about three-quarters full. "I don't know. Maybe we can get up to one of those cracks above, where the light is coming in? Maybe the rock's loose up there and we can dig through."

"Seems like a waste of time."

"We can go back to the burned log and see if someone will come by with a rope, but that doesn't seem promising, either. I haven't seen anyone but asshole Travis all morning."

He rubbed a hand under his chin. "Fair point. Let's see what we've got this way."

We ventured into the freaky side canyon, ten feet wide and thirty feet tall. Unlike the main slot canyon we'd come from, the walls weren't sheer. It was much more like the inside of a cave, with rocky outcroppings and nooks and crannies. But there didn't seem to be any way to claw through the top to return us to ground level. Uneasiness thumped in my chest. I started to seriously consider the possibility that we would have to spend the night here, hoping someone would find us.

Halfway down the length of the cave, I found a hole above where a shaft of light stabbed at the ground. I paused underneath it, examining the light shaft. After ogling it for a few seconds, I realized we weren't in a cave, but a slot canyon where the two sides had collapsed together.

Pug stood next to me, tugging on his chin. "I don't think we can get up there. These walls aren't good for climbing."

"I think you're probably right. What do you suggest?"

He sighed and rotated in a circle, then his face curled into a frown. "I have no idea. This sucks. This really, really, sucks."

Something caught my eye, a few dozen feet past the shaft of light. At first, I'd thought it was another one of the larger cairns, but this was something else. Near the ground, a hole in the rock, about two feet tall and three feet wide.

I pointed. "Maybe that."

Pug walked over to it and then leaned down. He stuck his head inside, and then a moment later pulled it back out. A glint of hope on his face. "I can feel a breeze. This does lead somewhere."

A creeping tension worked its way up my back, but I joined him next to the hole and peered inside it. "This might be a terrible idea. I'm not crazy about small and dark spaces."

"I think this is the best we have, though. We can't sit around, waiting for someone to rescue us."

"No," I said, shaking my head, "that's probably not going to happen soon."

We both stared at the hole, neither wanting to enter it. At least a full minute oozed by, both of us frozen with indecision.

"Freshman year at Oklahoma State," I said. "Do you remember when we were at the U and you hopped up on that copier and broke it?"

Pug snorted. "Yeah. Not as durable as they look."

"That's when I knew for sure you were gay."

His brow furrowed. "What was gay about that?"

"It wasn't that jumping up on the copier was gay. It was that I could tell you were doing it to impress the guy from New York. The sophomore with the long hair."

"Ahh, yeah," Pug said, a twinkle in his eye as he tilted his head back a little. "*That* guy. But, if you've known for, like, the last five years, why didn't you ever say anything?"

I shrugged. "I figured you'd tell me when you were ready."

He nodded, patted me on the shoulder, and we went back to staring at the hole. Thirty more seconds slipped by in silence.

"You want to go first?" he said.

I shook my head, so he held out his left hand, flat-palmed. He then made a fist with his right, hovering above his open palm.

I mirrored his movements, and we pumped our fists twice. On the third pump, I chose scissors, and he picked paper. I won.

Pug rolled his eyes and dropped to the ground. He crawled inside the opening, using his phone's flash as a light. We'd left our headlamps back at the campsite. There had been no spelunking on the agenda for today.

Once his frame was all the way inside, I followed, using his light as a guide. Plus, I wanted both hands free. I could barely see anything.

Each time I moved, some part of my body bumped up against a wall or loose rock. I was going to be sore after all this.

We spent three or four minutes crawling along at a slow pace. Pushing, fighting the tightness of the space. Soon, the path inside this crevice began to rise. I could feel cool air shifting toward us, like a breeze.

"You always do scissors," he said. "I should have known."

After a couple more minutes, we saw the first bit of light up ahead. Pug shielded his phone against his chest to get a good look at it. As the tunnel continued to rise, there was a light source up ahead. A way out.

"Let's move," I said. "I can see it."

He shined his light forward and picked up the pace. That's when the first pebbles plunged from the top of the tunnel to the floor. At first, it was only grains here and there. Then, a rock the size of a softball dislodged and smacked Pug in the back. He grunted but pushed on.

After another two minutes, the tunnel flattened out. I'd not felt paralyzed by my anxiety so far in the tunnel, but right then, it occurred to me that we had no way to turn around. If we came to a dead end, or the tunnel became too thin to pass, we would have no choice but to back out, feet first. For some reason, that made my heart thud. My mouth dried up, clamoring for a sip of the bourbon back at the campsite.

Pug must have sensed it too because he crawled even faster. And maybe that's why he didn't foresee the big rock poised to fall on him.

CHAPTER TWENTY-ONE

OKLAHOMA - NOW

I dream of sand. Sand and pink rocks like fields of dead flowers. An endless march of dried riverbeds dusted with gravel. Blue skies overhead and punishing morning cold giving way to dry heat in the afternoon. And of a hiking trail, alone, separated from my friend. Wondering if he's okay. He's been injured, but he refuses to concede. And I worry it will be the death of him.

As I ascend from the depths of an arid valley up a slope of rocks marked with cairns, a giant structure of rock appears before me. It's like a triangular building sent from an alien race, dropped into the middle of this desert. I'm awe-struck, standing before the towering monstrosity. I can't comprehend how such a thing could have happened.

And I think it will be the death of me, too.

In those moments between sleep and waking, it's like

flipping between two television channels so fast they blur together. Sunlight pours in through the curtains of the bedroom. The bed is shimmying, which doesn't do much for my stomach. The RV is in motion. When I look over to the floor, Nashoba's bag of drugs and guns is no longer there.

Funny, they let me sleep through the night. When I open the bedroom door, I see Dichali on the couch, covered with a blanket. Ash on a cot, next to that couch. Cassidy is driving, and Poppa Bear is in the passenger seat, head back, snoring away.

Cassidy cranes her neck and waves me forward. Head pounding, mouth full of nasty cheap whiskey muck, I plod along the interior of the moving vehicle. Have to carefully step over Ash's cot, and then I kneel on the floor, behind Cassidy.

"How do you feel this morning?" she says.

"Like a bear crapped in my ears."

She giggles. "Sounds about right. I should have warned you about drinking after a sweat."

"I thought you guys were going to wake me up."

"We tried a few hours ago, but you were zonked. Like a corpse."

"Sorry, I didn't mean to hog your bed. How long have we been on the road?"

"Not long. Maybe an hour."

Poppa Bear implied we would drive through the night,

so I shouldn't be surprised that he broke that promise. We're still on track to get me home by tonight, though.

"Are you ready for breakfast?" she asks. "There's a diner up ahead in Woodward we always stop at when we're in the area. They do a breakfast burrito so big you have to hold it with two hands. It's one of the most delicious things in the world, and you're going to have to take my word on that."

I picture a massive burrito, slathered with beans and cheese, and my stomach turns. But, I would like for the world to stop moving, and we have to park the RV for that to happen. "Sure, sounds good to me."

Poppa Bear snorts and turns on his side. A bit of drool leaking from the edge of his lip and fading into his beard. Ash sits up, like a bolt of lightning. Eyes wide open. He's frozen there, not moving. Then, his mouth creaks in a yawn, and he runs a hand through his long hair. He casts a neutral look at me and then hops out of the cot.

Over the next fifteen minutes, everyone else aboard the RV wakes up, visits the bathroom, takes turns splashing sink water on their faces. We all barely say ten words to each other. A smattering of *good mornings*, but it's quiet in the RV. Not any Grateful Dead pumping through the speakers yet. Ash makes coffee, and the pot disappears within a few minutes.

I'm camped out by the faucet, downing water to alleviate my hangover. I'm twenty-eight years old, and I only started getting hangovers about four or five years ago. In high school and college, I could pound drinks all night and wake up feeling refreshed and ready to go the next morning. Still, I almost never get them as bad as this, but I also don't usually drink bottom-shelf liquor like Old Crow. And I don't endure intense sessions inside sweat lodges, either.

When we pull over at the diner, my stomach is grateful the RV has stopped moving. Everyone files out of the side door, hands up to block out the sun. They must all be hungover too because even after the wake-up routine and coffee, we've all still said only a handful of words to each other.

It's Wednesday. I have three full days to return to Denver without causing any drama with Gavin Belmont. Poppa Bear promised to get me home tonight.

But, I can't help thinking of the bag I found late last night in the bedroom. Ashkii's bag of goodies. If these people are who I think they are, it's not a good idea for me to be around them. If we run into any nosy police officers, we're all going to jail. Or, maybe worse, if Ash and Dichali decide they don't want to go to jail, and then start waving that shotgun around in the face of some highway patrol officer.

But where am I supposed to go? I'm still broke, and still can't use public transportation without Gavin potentially finding out about it. I suppose I could call Frank and tell him the whole story, but I'm not sure if that's a good idea. The ex-cop seems like a good guy, but I honestly don't know him well. Confessing my road trip to him might be a terrible idea.

I blink, and Cassidy is standing in front of me. Everyone else has gone inside the diner, but we're out here in the parking lot, in the chilly country air. There's so much on my mind, I feel like I'm floating through everything this morning, sitting on a cloud above it all.

"You okay?" she says.

"Last night, I saw something. Ash's bag."

She nods. "Okay, what about it?"

"Do you know what's in there?"

"I do. It's nothing you need to worry about. Nothing bad is going to happen to you, Micah. We're good people."

She leans in to kiss me, but I pull back. My eyes flick toward the window of the diner. I don't see any of our road trip buddies, but still, my heart's racing.

"What?" she says.

"Don't you think that's dangerous? You're married, and your husband is right inside that building. A building with windows. I mean, I haven't had a chance to process how guilty I feel about sleeping with a married woman yet because there seems to be a much more immediate threat."

"You're being a drama queen."

"But still, what we did last night was wrong. I've never done anything like that before."

"Stop," she says. "Everything is fine. If you're worried about Poppa Bear, don't be. We swing. You and me didn't do anything in that teepee I wouldn't tell him about myself."

This catches me off guard, and I'm not sure how to feel about it. I suppose it does change things.

"You're still on the fence," she says.

I don't know what to say, so I stare at her.

"You want to take off. I can tell."

I hesitate and then after a few seconds, nod in agreement. Maybe I shouldn't tell her these things, but I already spilled my entire life story to her last night, so a little more information about what's going on with me won't change the situation much.

She casts a look back at the diner, and we watch our three companions settle into a booth. Picking up laminated menus from the table.

"He didn't want to bring you along," she says. "Poppa Bear. I had to talk him into it."

"I know. Thank you for that. I was in a desperate situation, and I kinda still am."

She steps closer to me. Her face is pained, her lower lip quivering. "If you go, take me with you."

"What?"

"I'm not asking to move in with you and become your girlfriend or anything like that, but I don't want you to disappear. There's something about you, Micah. I want to go with you if you go."

I turn my palms up toward the sky, speechless. If she's so sure everything with these guys is safe, why is she eager to sneak off with me? It doesn't make any sense. Take her with me? To what end? We barely know each other.

"Just think on it," she says.

Before I can think of something to say, my phone buzzes in my pocket. I slip it out to see a call from an unavailable number, but I know who it is. The person I've been dreading another call from since I began this stupid journey two days ago.

"I need to get this," I say, holding up the phone. "Sorry, it's important."

She shrugs and mopes toward the restaurant. I answer the call as I hold the phone up to my ear. Cassidy turns back to cast longing eyes at me, and it pierces my heart for a moment. She's beautiful, like the sort of woman I wouldn't think I'd be able to get. And that fact makes me angry at myself because I know it's clouding my judgment.

"Hello?"

"Micah," Gavin says, "how are you?"

"Um, good. How are you?"

"Busy. Always busy." He pauses. "What's going on with you? There's something in your tone."

"I don't know what you mean."

I can hear him grumbling on the other end of the line. "You're keeping your nose clean, right? There isn't anything I need to know about?"

"No. Everything is fine. Why are you calling me?"

"I wanted to give you a heads-up on something. I said I was going to be in town on Saturday? Well, I'm booked for a flight to Seattle on Saturday now, so I need to move things up a little."

"Move things up? What does that mean?"

"It means I'm going to be in Denver on Friday. Late Friday morning. I'll swing by as soon as I get there and we'll grab some food."

CHAPTER TWENTY-TWO

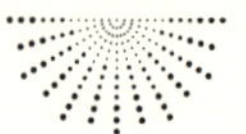

OKLAHOMA - NOW

I've spent the last hour sitting at the table in the RV, convincing myself it's fine that Gavin will arrive at Denver in less than forty-eight hours. I have to crack a window when they all decide to start passing around a weed pipe. Even Poppa Bear, who is driving, takes a few puffs. I'm not a fan of driving while intoxicated. Don't think it's a good idea. Yes, I got behind the wheel after having a few beers in Kansas two days ago, but I was not drunk, and I wasn't exactly a willing participant in that car chase on the highway.

The stench of their pot smoke drives me to lean my head toward the window, staring out at the trees and shrubs and farms and telephone lines whisking by. In this part of the state, the trend seems to be putting tractor tire pieces on the ground on either side of the driveway into your farm. I wonder how that became popular. Do they get together at town hall meetings to discuss?

The RV slows, and I blink to see it pulling into a rest stop. I have no idea where we are. Some random, non-city highway with nothing recognizable.

"What's up?" I say to my fellow passengers.

"Gotta take a dump," Poppa Bear says, bellowing it from the driver's seat. In the passenger seat, Cassidy grins at me, rolling her eyes. Dichali and Ash are on the couch, playing some game together, both on their phones. Heavy-lidded, blood-streaked eyes.

There's a bathroom in the RV, so I don't know why we're pulling over, but I don't ask. Everyone files out of the vehicle to a rest stop that looks eerily like the one from two days ago where I engaged in the confrontation with those two rednecks. Gravel, picnic table, brick building. Wide open space on all sides of the turnout.

For a moment, I panic. But this can't be Kansas. No way we've driven that far. And it's not even in the right direction. I-135 would be significantly out of the way unless Poppa Bear outright lied to me about our travel route.

I squint at the rest stop entrance and see a tiny Oklahoma state seal on the sign. Not Kansas. Feel a little silly for thinking it, but this has been a week of silliness. Not good silliness, but the kind that makes it hard to believe all of this is real.

Poppa Bear and Cassidy head for the restrooms while

Ash walks along a fence nearby. Dichali climbs on top of a nearby bench and opens a pack of cigarettes. A few cars whiz by on the road behind us, but there's no one else at the rest stop. Strikes me how different my home state is to downtown Denver, where I live now. Technically, "LoDo," but it's the same thing. And that difference is how it's possible to be alone out here in the vast Oklahoma flatlands. You can stretch out and have space all to yourself.

"Micah," Dichali says. When I look at him, he waves me over. He lights the cigarette and grins at me when I join him next to the picnic table. Finally, I get a good look at his neck tattoo. It's the wings and head of a bird, with the lower half below his collar line. But, now that I can see it close-up, the individual pieces of the bird are made up of tiny people, linked together. It's an intricate, well-done piece of artwork.

"Like the ink?" he says as he puffs the cigarette. Right away, I notice it smells odd. Like chemicals. He holds it out to me.

I lift my hands. "No thanks, I don't smoke."

"Oh, it's not a regular cigarette. It's a *stick*."

"A what?"

"A cigarette that's been dipped in *water*."

I cock my head. "I'm not following you."

"Water is like PCP, but without the heady come-down part."

"I don't really get into that stuff. I'm a regular bourbon kind of guy."

His face darkens. "Think you're better than me because you're straight-edge?"

"What? No. I didn't mean to offend you or anything. I'm just not into that stuff."

His scowl loosens, and he shrugs like he's about to say *your loss*, but he doesn't get the words out because Ash comes marching in our direction, hair swinging and hands balled at his sides.

"What the hell are you doing?" Ash says to Dichali.

"I'm not doing anything. Ease up, Ash."

Ash glares at me. "You're going to share our sticks with him?"

"What's the problem?" Dichali says. "I'm only being neighborly. We've got plenty enough to share."

Seems like this is a good place for me to interject. "Hey, it's cool. I'm not into that stuff, anyway, so you don't have to worry about me. I don't want any of your stash."

As soon as this last word leaves my mouth, I know it's a mistake. Ash and Dichali both eye me. It occurs to me I don't know who came into the RV's bedroom while I was sleeping and removed the bag of guns and drugs. Maybe it was Cassidy, or maybe it was one of these two. Perhaps they assume I've seen everything inside it.

Ash advances in my direction. "What did you say, white boy?"

"Let's take a breath here," I say. "We're all getting worked up over nothing. I don't want to smoke a stick, I don't care that you're smoking sticks, and now everybody knows it. Like it never happened. No harm done."

But Ash takes another step toward me, brushing up against the picnic table. Sneering so hard he's now baring his teeth. Dichali does nothing, puffing on his chemical cigarette, staring blankly at the two of us.

At that moment, Poppa Bear emerges from the bathroom, wiping his hands on his pants. Right after him comes Cassidy. Both of them, frowning, hustle toward the picnic table.

"What's going on out here?" Cassidy says.

Ash leans toward me and places four fingers on my chest. Gives me a shove. Not hard enough to knock me off my feet, but I do move a step back. He raises his hand again, and it takes everything in me to resist. I know exactly what to do: I can slip my thumb into his palm and wrap my hand around his hand, perpendicular to it. This gives me options. If I'm on the inside of his arm, I'll have all the leverage at my disposal. I can twist it toward the outside of his body, making him turn to his right. Or, I can twist it to the inside of his body, making him pivot to his left. Either way leaves one side of his face exposed, and I can easily crack his jaw with my free fist. As big and tough as this shithead is, he's not more powerful than leverage.

But I don't exercise my knowledge. The last thing I want is for this situation to explode everywhere like the C4 they're smuggling in their magic bag. I still think I can salvage this and get home on time. Especially now I know that 'on time' is a day shorter than I thought it was.

If they strand me out here, the situation only gets worse.

"There's something you're not telling us," Ash says.

"Maybe so, but whatever I'm not telling you is none of your damn business. We're all just passengers here, so there's no need for your aggression."

He gets in my face, and I know mouthing off to him was a mistake, but I couldn't help it. I raise my arms to get everyone's attention. "Let's all take a step back. Everything is fine."

But Cassidy doesn't listen. She inserts herself between Ash and me, facing off against him. Her chin up, mean-mugging him.

"You better move, woman," Ash says.

Poppa Bear, off to the side, steps in. "Cass and Ash, that's enough. We're not going to have another squabble like Little Rock." He grabs hold of Cassidy's bare arm. His fingers sink into her flesh, and she grimaces.

"Hey," I say to him as he pulls Cassidy away. "Let go of her."

Poppa Bear glares at me. Ash glares at me. Dichali, his eyes glassy and a drug-fueled grin on his face, stares off into space.

"It's okay, Micah," Cassidy says. She wriggles free of Poppa Bear's grasp. "It's all okay. No big deal." She holds up her arm to show me she's fine, but I can see the fear on her face.

I flash back to her asking me, only an hour or two ago, to take her with me if I leave. She's terrified of him, despite what she says.

Poppa Bear, thumbs hooked in the belt loops on his jeans, clears his throat. "Everyone back on the RV. Got a couple more hours 'til our next stop, and we don't have time for this in-fighting bullshit."

Dichali hops off the picnic table, wobbling as he walks toward our house on wheels. Cassidy and Poppa Bear next.

Finally, Ash inches closer toward me. "Watch your step, Micah. I know you wanted to hit me just then. I hope you're prepared to find out what happens if you do."

CHAPTER TWENTY-THREE

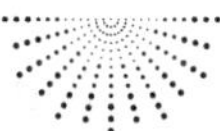

UTAH - FOUR YEARS AGO

I'd seen the chunk of the boulder, dangling there above Pug's head, as he crawled underneath it. Like a stalactite reverse iceberg, jutting from the roof of the tunnel. Pointed at the tip. He barely passed under it without scraping his back on it. I couldn't see much since I was using the flashlight on Pug's phone as my only source of light, and the shadows bounced in all directions as he held it out while crawling forward.

I didn't even know what it was until he was already full underneath it.

And then it shifted. The piece I could see was the size of a basketball, but I soon realized it was bigger than that. Pug's torso was directly beneath it when it started to rumble and give way.

He paused and shifted his hips, trying to look around. The light from his flashlight bounced off the walls of our cave tunnel. Bits of smaller rock trickled down, showering both of us with sandy pebbles.

Then the basketball fell. Except, as it dislodged, I could see that it was sized more like a watermelon. This giant rock broke loose and dove the two-foot distance from the tunnel ceiling right onto the back of Pug's leg. I heard it smack his calf, then he screamed. His hiking boot, twelve inches in front of me, jiggled.

"What the hell is that?" he said, in hysterics. "Holy shit, what is that? Did something bite me?"

I lurched forward as close as I could. The rock blocked most of the light from Pug's phone. "It's a piece of the tunnel ceiling. It fell. Hang on, Pug. I'll move it off you."

"Is the tunnel going to fall on us?"

"I don't know," I said as I tried to push even closer. His hiking boot was in the way, a big high-top thing. I couldn't raise above it to get a good grasp on the rock.

"Hurry. It hurts like hell." He grunted, breathing through clenched teeth. I extended my arms, placed two hands on the rock, and then tried to shift it to the right. It barely budged an inch. And when I couldn't push it any further, it settled again, and Pug yelped.

Panic set in. I didn't have the strength or the free space to heave it off his leg.

Crazy thoughts appeared in my head. Like taking out my Springfield and shooting it. Or letting Pug twist his leg until it broke his bones so he could be more flexible.

Cutting his leg off like the movie about the guy trapped under the boulder in that canyon.

I needed a plan, but my pulse was thudding in my ears, and I couldn't think.

Pug groaned and tried to scurry free, but his leg was pinned. "Michael, please do something. I can't even turn around. How big is this thing?"

"Pretty big. Big enough that there's not enough space for me to roll it off on either side. There's only an inch or two of clearance on the sides."

"You have to do something. I can't move forward or back, and I can't get my hands down there. Do something, please."

My head buzzed with adrenaline. The pressure of the moment wanted to overwhelm me.

I had to fix this. But I had no idea how. Then, it occurred to me that if this section could fall, the rest of the tunnel might collapse on us at any moment.

"Mikey, help me."

"I can't think. I don't know what to do. There's not enough space for me to shift it off you. If I have to rock it back and forth, I'm afraid I'll crush your leg."

"Shit," he said, and I could hear the agony in his voice. The pain was getting worse.

An idea formed. Maybe I was thinking about this in the wrong dimension. "Wait. Shine your light back here."

He shifted the phone over his head and pointed the light back toward me. There were only a few inches on either side, but there were several inches of clearance between the top of the rock and the roof of the tunnel.

"It's going to have to go up," I said.

"Can you lift it?"

"I don't see any other way to move this thing. After I lift it, you have to jerk your leg forward, okay? I'll give you a three count."

Panting, breathless, he grunted his acknowledgment. I scooted forward, pressing my body against the tunnel roof to clear Pug's hiking boot. I dug my heels in and pushed until my head thumped against the rock, with Pug's hiking boot beneath my chest. Then, I shimmied my arms along the walls of the tunnel until they were wrapped around the rock.

I laced my arms around it, hugging it. The cold and gritty surface pressed against my face. I squeezed, feeling the heft of the rock. This thing was solid; I didn't know if I could do it. I didn't know what it weighed, but it felt enormous.

But I had to. There wasn't another option. Either I moved it, or we both died when this tunnel weakened and then collapsed on us.

"Ready?"

"Yes," he groaned. "Please hurry."

"Okay. One, two, three."

I braced my abs and squeezed my arms around the rock as tightly as possible. Then I arched my back and pushed up. Pressed my feet against the tunnel roof for a little extra leverage.

A grunt turned into a roar as I threw everything I had into lifting it.

And the rock shifted, just a fraction of an inch.

Pug yelled as he tried to scoot forward. I raised my chest, so I wasn't trapping his foot underneath me. Back aching, arms vibrating from the exertion. My biceps felt like they were about to pop out of my arms, my shoulder sockets strained to the breaking point.

And I felt his foot slip forward.

"Okay!" he shouted.

I let go of the rock, and it thudded onto the floor, then rolled over toward me. I pushed out to keep it from smacking me in the face.

"You okay?"

"I'm bleeding," he said. "My leg feels all wet."

"How bad?"

"I don't know. Can you get over the rock or are you stuck back there?"

He lifted his phone above his head again and shone the light back here. The rock was lying flat on the tunnel floor, leaving eight or nine inches of clearance above it.

"It's going to be tight." In other circumstances, Pug would have made a snarky comment about my mother right after me saying something like that. But, if it even occurred to him, he didn't say a word about it.

I pushed myself up, scraping the roof of the tunnel, and lurched forward. The rock ground against my chin as I pushed past it. First my chest, where I could feel it tearing my shirt. Then my torso, and then I was on the other side of it. Splashes of Pug's blood transferred from the rock to me and slicked my chest and stomach. When I bumped into his feet, I stopped. Panting, head pounding, arms numb from the superhuman exertion of freeing Pug's trapped foot.

"I'm clear."

"Thank the Flying Spaghetti Monster," he said, and I could hear the pain and exhaustion in his voice. But, even so, we still had to get out. And, we had no idea how much further we had to go.

We didn't wait long. Pug resumed pushing forward, letting out a grunt any time his injured leg shifted. I could feel the slickness of his blood on the tunnel floor. Could hear his leg scraping against the tunnel. Sounded like he wasn't able to bend his leg at all.

I had visions of his calf being flattened like a pancake. Couldn't see the damage from here. He didn't stop to let me examine it. We were both focused only on getting the hell out of here as soon as possible.

After another five minutes of no words and only grunts, the tunnel climbed again. As soon as it did, we could both see the exit. The tunnel ended in a shaft of light in front of a small pile of rocks. The light hit my eyes, blinding me for a second.

As we neared it, the roof of the tunnel grew taller, and I

could crouch instead of crawl. As Pug pushed himself up, I could now see his leg. The calf was a bloody mess, his foot at a slightly awkward angle.

He tried to crouch, but gave a yelp and resumed crawling. Closer to the shaft of light, I was able to rise to my feet, and I wrapped an arm around Pug's shoulders. Helped him move along to the rocks, which now resembled a set of stairs. One side of his body moved with no trouble, but the other side was useless. Like dragging a dead body.

When we reached the pile of rocks, Pug slipped away from my arms and thudded to a seat on the tunnel floor. I kicked at the rocks, and they crumbled away, letting in more light. Beams of light appeared as the rocks fell away from the cave entrance on this side. Through the holes, I saw more boulders, grass, and rock spires in the distance.

I pushed through. My aching hands pulled me up the rocks until I was beyond the tunnel. I looked around to see a flat slick rock surface. Had no idea where we were.

I turned around and reached back into the tunnel to grab Pug's hands, and then pulled him out. When he got to his feet, he staggered and then steadied himself. Calf purple with bruises, streams of blood turning it into a candy cane.

"Thank you," he said, chest heaving. His face and clothes were covered in sand and dust. He tried to steady himself on his feet, then he sank down onto the rock below us. He grunted as he shifted his foot forward.

"Okay?" I said.

"I think so. Doesn't feel broken."

"Let me see," I said as I bent down to examine it.

"What do you think, Dr. McBriar? What does your college-dropout medical training say to you?"

I frowned at him. "Well, it didn't break your smart-ass bone."

He shifted, grimacing. Spent a few seconds trying to rotate his foot. After a couple tries, he could make it swivel, then he extended it. He pointed his toes, which brought a whimper to his lips.

I snatched my water bottle and had a sip. "Any idea where we are?"

He crawled a few feet along the rock surface and pointed. "We're at the edge of Chesler. Our campsite is over there."

I stood next to him, eying the flat, grassy space between us and our campsite. "When we get back, we'll pack up our stuff and go. I've had enough."

Pug glared at me, fire in his eyes. "No. This fucker Travis is going to answer for what he's done."

CHAPTER TWENTY-FOUR

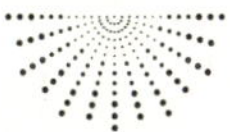

OKLAHOMA - NOW

Cassidy leaves the passenger seat chair and sits with me at the table for a few minutes, both of us in silence. The RV rolls on. No one else notices her transition because they're too busy singing along to some angry, thrashing music. Dichali picked the playlist this time. Sounds like what a sullen and rebellious teenager might choose to listen to while skulking around his room.

She makes eyes at me, smiling and flirting, and I try to offer it back to her, but there's too much on my mind. The shoebox is in the pantry, stuffed behind the boxes of cereal. I don't know where Ash's bag of mayhem is, but it's ever-present in my thoughts.

Also, I can see the bruise left by Poppa Bear's fingerprints on her arm. Like five purple circles on her milky flesh. I feel guilty that I didn't pop him in the face the second he grabbed her like that. But what would it have accomplished? Would it have changed him for the better? Would it have made Cassidy wake up to the abusive cycle she likely lives inside?

Ten or fifteen more minutes of silence elapse. Next time Cassidy gets up to use the bathroom, she returns to her chair up at the front afterward. Maybe she thinks I'm cold on purpose. That I'm not interested in her. I don't know what to say to alleviate her fear, so I say nothing, and leave her to wonder what's in my head.

She asked me to take her with me. I can't do that, can I?

After a couple hours, the RV slows. I finally look out the window to see a wooded area, with a dirt road cutting through it. Barbed wire on either side of the road. A sign ahead reads *William and Sons Recreational Vehicle and Trailer Park.*

"What is this?" I say.

Poppa Bear turns down the music as the RV rattles and shakes on the bumpy road. "Trailer park," he says. "We're going to make a quick stop. It'll be lickety-split, and we'll be done before you know it."

That's what they said yesterday in the state park, and we ended up spending the night. Since Cassidy is in the kitchen, making sandwiches, I raise a hand to get her attention. "We're not camping out here, are we?"

She shakes her head. "No, this will be quick. Ash and Dichali have some business with the guy who runs the place. Then we'll rest a little and be on our way."

Her words don't set my mind at ease. The way Ash and Dichali stare at me as I ask my questions doesn't set my mind at ease, either.

I check the time on my phone. It's already late afternoon. I have no desire to push too far up against the deadline for my return to Denver, and not just for Gavin. I've missed three days of work now and was hoping to show up at Frank's office tomorrow. Maybe I should call him, but somehow, I dread talking to him even more than I do Gavin. Gavin's an asshole. Frank is a nice old man so I would have a hard time explaining my current situation without slathering the conversation with lies.

Poppa Bear slides the RV into a spot along the grass, in what looks like a campsite. There is a circle of lawn chairs with an umbrella providing shade above them. Poppa Bear aligns the RV's gas tank with a thing that looks like a smaller version of a gas pump. He steps out of the car and hooks up a hose from the thing to a panel on the RV. Must be charging it.

"Let's go," Cassidy says. We all file out of the RV, and the afternoon heat and humidity prickle my skin immediately. In this park, there are a dozen RVs in slots like this one, all in a row against a barbed wire fence. On the other side are the trailer homes, in rows like little city blocks. Maybe thirty of them. We're in a clearing inside what looks like endless woods on three sides. The fourth side is a hill, with a large house atop it.

Like a little community, complete with streets. I watch

a man and a woman heave fishing poles over their shoulders as they walk toward the woods. Each carrying a beer bottle in their free hands. I lick my lips. Could use a drink.

Dichali pauses in front of me, then he raises his eyebrows to get my attention. He points at the house on the hill. "We're going up there. You stay here and mind your own business. Cassidy can keep you company."

I blink a few times, staring at him.

"You get all that?" he says.

"I'm supposed to stay here."

Dichali nods and Ash hitches his bag over his shoulder. My heart thumps. I have visions of them going up to the house and rigging it with explosives. I assumed they're drug dealers, but what if they're urban terrorists or something more dangerous?

Should I do something about it? At least find out their plan?

"What are you doing at that house?" I say and immediately regret it. The air seems to grow thick, and everyone present gives me a strange look.

Ash gets in my face. "Why do you want to know?"

I shrug and say nothing.

"I don't know who you are," he says, venom in his eyes. "And I don't know why you're with us. And, I don't know why I should let you question me like you have any idea what's going on here. You've been too curious since the moment we met you yesterday."

I look around at the others for a little backup. Dichali

and Poppa Bear are standing off to the side, arms crossed. Seem content not to intervene.

"I don't want any trouble," I say. "I'm just trying to hitch a ride to Denver."

Ash swishes his lips around, eyes darting back and forth across my face. "I don't think we're going to let you hang around any longer. You're going to stay here. You can find another ride to Denver."

Cassidy gasps and tries to step in. I hold up my hand to wave her off. I don't want another incident with Poppa Bear trying to forcibly remove her from the situation like the rest stop this morning.

"You can't do that," I say.

He spits on the ground. "The hell I can't."

"Ash, come on," Poppa Bear says, shaking his head. "He doesn't mean any harm."

He steps closer and lets the bag slip down his shoulder, so it's resting on his forearm. It's at the perfect distance for him to reach his other arm across and slip inside it. But, it's still zippered shut. If he tries to make a move, I'll have time. The bag is heavy enough that if I give his shoulder a quick shove, the weight of it should knock him to the ground.

But, if I do that, if I live through whatever comes next, they will most definitely leave me stranded here. That's the best case scenario. Worst case, cops will show up. Then, it's game over.

"How did he know about us?" Ash says, looking at me

but speaking to Poppa Bear.

"I didn't," I say. "They found me at Joe's in Stillwater."

Ash tilts his head a little toward Poppa Bear. "That true?"

As Poppa Bear nods his answer, I put my hands up. "This is all getting too serious. I'm just a guy, trying to get a ride back to Denver. I don't want to get all up in your business. That's not how I do things."

Ash grits his teeth and narrows his eyes at me. "Bullshit. You're a nosy bitch."

I bite my lip and tell myself to keep quiet, but I can't help it. This guy isn't as tough as he thinks he is. It's getting on my nerves. "You need to be careful what you say to me."

While my gaze is on Ash and his bag of goodies, Cassidy steps in. "Stop this. Right now. Micah is our guest, and I don't want you to talk to him that way."

Ash sneers at her. "Who are you to give me orders, woman?"

"Easy, Ashkii," Poppa Bear says. "That's my wife you're talking to."

The gravity in Poppa Bear's tone seems to get through to Ash. He takes a step back and then nods at Poppa Bear.

"We'll be back in a while," Ash says to me, "why don't you spend your free time thinking about your curiosity, and what it did to the cat."

And then, the three men leave us there, headed for the house on the hill.

CHAPTER TWENTY-FIVE

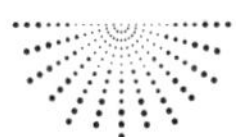

OKLAHOMA - NOW

As soon as they're out of sight, Cassidy tries to kiss me, but I pull back. "Sorry. I need a few minutes."

"Don't leave."

"Huh?"

Her eyes implore me. "Please, don't leave yet. I know you want to, but please don't run off into the woods."

"Why?"

She frowns and has no answer for me. After a pause, she turns toward the interior of the RV park and leaves me be. I wait another moment or two, thinking through my options. Being here, with these people, has become an untenable situation. I'm not sure if all of us will survive the rest of the trip.

I've been too passive so far, putting up with all kinds of shit in the name of safe passage back to Denver. But is it awful for me to leave Cassidy here, with them, when she's already asked to come with me?

I don't know what to do. Throat's dry, I need a drink.

I board the RV and uncap a fifth of whiskey from the cabinet above the fridge. I didn't ask for permission, but I barely give any shits anymore. The liquid slides down my throat as I gulp a few inches in one swallow. Immediately, I feel better.

I unearth my shoebox from its hiding spot. My now-steady hands guide it to the table and lift the lid. The first thing sitting on the top is the picture of me and my best friend, at the Riverwalk in OKC. Taken only a few weeks before his death. Underneath that, the selfie of both of us in Canyonlands National Park. This picture almost amuses me, despite the circumstances surrounding our reason for the visit there. Him, looking so suave. Me, looking sloppy and haggard. At the beginning of a multi-day descent into desert hell.

Below that, there rests the fabled wolf's head business card and two flash drives. One of them contains music my friend gave to me. The other, some spreadsheets, although I've never understood what for. He didn't have a chance to tell me before he died.

Below those things is a sea of old letters and other memorabilia. Concert ticket stubs. A piece of a paper clip, folded into a triangle, given to me by a high school girlfriend. I have no idea why I kept it, but it had serious significance at the time. Probably a symbol of our enduring love. We did tend to take ourselves too seriously in high school.

I wonder, for a moment, what the old girlfriend is up to these days. Probably married with kids, working a regular job somewhere. Maybe even moved away from Oklahoma, something we used to talk about. If I weren't banned by WitSec from logging onto social media, I could easily look her up and find out.

She's probably not waiting in an RV owned and operated by a volatile crew of drug hustlers.

I should go. Cut my losses and wander off to find another way home. Some non-homicidal maniacs to give me a ride to Denver.

But what about Cassidy?

What the hell are they doing up there in that house on the hill? Nothing good, that's for sure.

The temptation to explore burns at me.

I stow the shoebox and steel my nerves. Going to find answers.

I've got the knife stolen from one of the rednecks, and I can probably scour the RV and uncover another gun or six. But I'm not hiking up there to shoot up the place. Just for some information.

I have to know what's happening.

After another big slug of the whiskey, I leave the RV and meander through the trailer park, late afternoon sun sinking in the sky. Heart thumping against my chest. A few people are out, sitting on porches and plucking beer cans from coolers sloshing with ice water.

The house on the hill looms above the valley, a three-story thing that looks out of place here. Big, fancy. As I near it, though, I can see the chipped paint and the missing shutters on half the windows. Looks more like a haunted house than a luxury home.

Once I'm close, I drop to a crouch and remove the knife from my back pocket. Extend the blade and focus on a window near the side that could either be a kitchen or a living room. If they're not in one, they're probably in the other.

Foot over foot, my eyes on the glass, trying to steal a peek. And, once I'm within twenty feet, I can see a figure in the window. It's Poppa Bear's burly and hairy frame, his big beard shrouding his face. And then, standing next to him, Ash's long hair. Both of them are facing away from the window.

A little closer, I can see a ledge with a dish soap bottle. This is the kitchen. Staying low, I pass underneath the window. I can hear something through the glass. Mumbles, people talking, the sounds of things shifting around. Then, there's a moan.

Past the window, the house turns, and I follow the corner to see another window. From this angle, I now find Dichali, Ash, and Poppa Bear standing on one side of the kitchen, up against the sink.

And I note that Ash is holding a bloody rag, wrapped around his knuckles.

I lean a little closer to the window to spy what they're all looking at. And, in a chair opposite them is a man, seated. His body is tied to the chair with an orange extension cord binding his hands. He's got on beige coveralls and a green John Deere cap. Blood dripping from his lip. His chest is heaving, his lips sputtering as he's saying something I can't hear.

Ash asks him a question and the man shakes his head. In a flash, Dichali whips his hand forward, slashing across the man's face. I didn't see the knife before, but in an instant, he draws blood from the man's cheek. The bound man screams, trying to skirt away from them, but there's nowhere to go. A few splatters dot the walls behind him.

My eyes flick past the bleeding man. I can see through the door out of the kitchen, including a sliver of the stairs up to the second floor.

And there, I see a girl, cowering, looking over the banister into the scene in the kitchen. She can't be more than twelve years old. Short, thin, hair pulled into symmetrical pigtails at the base of her scalp.

Can they not see her from their spot in the kitchen? Was she hiding upstairs, and now she's come down to find out what's going on?

She must be this man's daughter or niece. There's an intensity on her face I can't quite categorize, but she's captivated by the activity in the kitchen.

The girl sees me, and her eyes widen.

I have to do something. I have to get her out of that house before Ash and the others spot her. They'll kill her for witnessing this scene. I'm sure of it.

With her gaze focused on me, I flick my head toward the front door, and she hesitates, but then nods. I duck down, back around the kitchen windows, toward the front of the house. When I reach the patio, I slink across, crouched. There's a 50/50 chance they'll hear this door open, if it's even unlocked.

Here we go.

I reach up a hand to try the knob and find it not locked. Turn it gently, taking care to limit the noise as much as possible. Then, I ease the door open, fast enough not to squeak, but not too fast. No idea if they can see the front door from here. If they're still wailing on the guy—and it sounds like they are—they might not even notice.

When the door is open about a foot, the little girl appears in the doorway. Staring at me. She looks angry, for some reason.

I wave her outside, using the other hand to put a finger to my lips. Inside, the hostage is now moaning, and someone is punching him. Working him over.

The girl continues to stare at me, frowning. She makes a face, and then she turns her head slightly, back toward the kitchen. Her mouth opens as she draws in a big breath.

She's about to scream.

I reach out and snatch her. Pull her to me, wrapping a

hand around her mouth. She does scream, but I manage to get my hand over her mouth before she can let it out. It's muffled and only as loud as a whisper against the palm of my hand.

I pull her outside and shut the door. She's kicking against me, trying to bite my hand. The door shuts a little harder than I intended. They probably heard it.

She's fighting as hard as she can, but since I have a hundred pounds on her, I sweep her into the air and hustle us to the side of the house. Keeping her tight against me. Her heels dig into my shins and my knees, and it takes everything I have not to drop her.

We press against the side of the house. A second later, the front door opens. I'm squeezing her, keeping her silent. She's not screaming anymore or kicking me. Now, she's moved on to jabbing her elbows against my rib cage. I brace my abs and take it, trying to keep her still. No idea why she's fighting me, but if Ash or Dichali or Poppa Bear comes out here and sees us, we're in for trouble. I'm outnumbered and have no desire to take on all three of them.

After a few more seconds, the door shuts again, and the girl relaxes.

"I'm going to let go of you," I say. "I am not here to hurt you, so please don't scream. You'll get us both killed."

When I release my grip, she jumps away from me, then plants her feet, turns, and spits in my face.

"How dare you," she says.

"How dare... what? I am so confused right now."

"This is kidnapping," she says, her little jaw flexing.

"Whoa, wait a second. I'm trying to *help* you, kid. Is that your dad in there?"

She nods. "You a buddy of his?"

"No. I've never seen him before. I know those guys beating the crap out of him, but they're no friends of mine."

She pauses, considering this. Her eyes dart over my face, searching. "Fine. How about you leave me alone now?"

"No, it's not fine. They're killing him in there. If they find you, they'll kill you too."

"I hope they do kill him," she says, sneering. "No-good piece of shit."

"What?"

"He'll get what he deserves on account of what he done. Whatever, I don't care. I'm going to my uncle's place. You can have him."

She digs a foot in the dirt and then struts off, down the hill. I watch her go, horribly confused. After a few more seconds, before she disappears down the hill, she turns and gives me the finger.

Weird.

What kind of a man is tied to the chair in the kitchen that his own daughter doesn't care about him being murdered? Who is this little girl that can be so cold about the whole thing?

As I creep back around the side of the house, I hear him scream again. This cry of pain is clear, and it only lasts a second or two. I spy through the window as Dichali slashes a blade against the man's neck, and his head lolls back and then forward. A curtain of red blanketing the front of his shirt.

They've killed him.

CHAPTER TWENTY-SIX

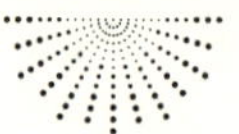

OKLAHOMA - NOW

I return to the RV and splash water on my face. The little girl's words about her dad deserving what happened to him rattle around in my brain like a guitar pick dropped through the sound hole. The image of his blood pouring down his neck floats before my face.

I set Boba Fett in the soap tray and stare at him. I've decided to go. Just pack up my few possessions and skip out of here as soon as possible. Damn the consequences, but I don't need to spend another day with these lunatic murderers.

Maybe the bound man in that house had it coming to him, or maybe he didn't. I'm honestly not interested in finding out one way or the other because I have enough of my own problems. Everything I've put up with so far to gain a ride home is no longer worth it. Whatever tipping point that existed has now been met.

"This is messed up," I say to Boba Fett. "That little girl from the house was in shock, right? She didn't know what she was saying. Couldn't have known what she was saying. Maybe I shouldn't have let her leave."

He says nothing, but I know what he means. Walking away from this is selfish. I need to check on that little girl and make sure she's okay.

I sigh and drop him back in my pocket. In the mirror behind me, Cassidy appears. She places a hand on the back of my neck. Her finger feels wet, as if she's recently washed her hands.

"You're tense," she says. "Turn around."

I face her, and she's looking up at me, trying to smile, but I can see the worry etched on her face. It's been a long day.

"Would you like me to relax you?" she asks.

"What do you mean?"

She licks her lips and tilts her head, throwing flirty eyes at me. Big and slick infinity pools of eyes that seem impossible to resist.

I take her hands inside mine. "I don't think I can do that right now."

"What's wrong? Did I do something?"

"Do you have any idea what's going on up in that house on the hill?"

She frowns. "Yeah. They're talking to someone who stole from us."

"*Talking* to him?"

"Maybe more. I didn't want to be a part of it. But it has to happen, so there's nothing I can do about it."

She tries again to put her spidery hands on me, and I shrink away. I can't tell her I'm leaving. If she knows what's going on in the house, then she's given her approval to it.

It has to happen, she said.

She's as malicious as they are, only in a much prettier package. These people are as bad as the ones I fled Oklahoma to escape. The ones who ripped up my life and dumped it in the trash can.

"I need to clear my head. I'm going to go for a walk."

She steps back and nods. "Sure, if you need to do that. But don't go too far okay? We're having dinner in a little bit. I'll make hot dogs."

"Okay, sure. Sounds good." I leave her there in the RV as I wander out into the lot. Resist the urge to telegraph my intentions by making any further eye contact with her. But I have no desire to stay for dinner.

I'm going to look for that pre-teen girl. If I can't find her by the time it gets dark, I intend to collect my shoebox and get the hell out of here. Damn the consequences of being stranded in Oklahoma with no way home. I'm not spending another night with these lunatic hippie drug dealer terrorists.

Not my circus. Not my monkeys.

A few cars shuffle along the grass, people outside their trailers flip burgers on barbecues. Little children play in sandboxes. Mangy dogs wander, sniffing trash cans and begging at the feet of humans with food.

I reach the edge of the woods, where there's a break in the barbed wire fence. I let my finger tap on one of the barbed points. It brings a smile of nostalgia to my face, which is followed by a pang of memory tickling my spine. Reminds me of the old and rusty fence on my grandfather's farm. How my brother and sister and I used to go out to collect the bits of horse hair that would catch in the barbs, like streamers. It seemed fun then. Most things seem fun when you're a little kid.

Past the fence, the foliage extends forever, like an endlessly looping video. Humongous pecan trees, and those bring back memories too. Shuffling through the shells on the ground among the autumn leaves.

But these trees overhead seem infested with webworms. Thick cocoons wrapping around clusters of branches, milky white like dense spiderwebs. They're parasites, not decoration. They'll take every bit of nutrients the trees have and then leave them for dead.

After ten more minutes of fruitless walking, I come upon a creek. It meanders along in a lazy squiggle, flowing from the hill, through the woods, and disappearing in some unseen path. I find a nearby downed log and sit, letting the sounds wash over me.

No twelve-year-old girl anywhere within eyesight. If she did run off to find her uncle, then there's a strong chance I'll never see her again.

I should go. But should I? Should I stay and try to help Cassidy?

I'm conflicted. Ash is a thug and a clear and present danger to everyone around him. I know his type. I used to deal with people like him all the time, back in my tenure with my former employer.

As I'm sitting here, the creek grows louder. I stare at it, and it's not rushing any faster, but it feels like someone has turned up the volume. Odd.

I could kill Ash. That might be the only way to keep him from harming the rest of them, which he will, eventually. His comment about my curiosity wasn't a warning, it was a prophecy. He wanted me to know I should leave now or he would slit my throat and throw me out the back of the RV, probably somewhere in New Mexico. Out in the desert where no one would care.

Maybe he'll do the same to Cassidy if she tried to stop him. Maybe leaving is the best way to keep her safe. But if I leave, or I hurt him and thus alienate the others, I'm stranded here. Will miss my rendezvous date with Gavin in Denver. What will Gavin do if he finds out I've left the state? Put me in a room somewhere and sweat me, yelling at me for hours? Revoke my Witness Protection? Send me back to prison?

A return to prison would be awful, but I'm not sure if leaving WitSec doesn't have its benefits, though. No more check-ins. No more US Marshals watching me, tracking my moves.

Gavin can be a real prick sometimes.

Of course, I would lose the aid of the US government. I would put myself potentially back into harm's way. I would still have to stay away from my parents and my siblings, for their own protection.

A strange sensation comes to the back of my head. I feel like my spine is tingling, but no, that's not the right word. It's like I can *feel* my spine. Like I'm looking at an x-ray where my spine is glowing in highlighted white. But I do not see it, I'm *feeling* it.

Maybe I'm dehydrated. I haven't had any water in hours.

"Is it money?" a voice says behind me. I turn to see Cassidy in a long dress, gliding as she shuffles through the leaves.

"What?" I say.

"The reason you're traveling with us. I know you didn't want to be here, in the RV with us. You didn't want to come along when we found you in Stillwater. I could see it on your face, like you were embarrassed and too proud to ask. So, I was wondering if it's because you didn't have the cash to buy a plane ticket."

"I don't have access to money, true."

She nods, and I notice the strangest thing. There's a glow to her like she's bathed in sunlight. But, the sun is behind us, and it's setting, almost down now.

I feel a chill along my back. A bead of sweat drips down from between my shoulder blades.

She sits on the log and then straddles it, facing me. She tilts her head back and lets out a little howl, a brief and staccato imitation of a wolf.

"Howl with me," she says.

I shake my head. I don't want to howl.

"That's fine," she says. "I can get money. There's a bus station in Guymon, and it's not that far from here. We can buy tickets to anywhere."

"You can get money? What does that mean?" As I say the words, they feel foreign coming out of my mouth. Like I'm hearing them on television, not *saying* them. It's weird.

And then, I realize how amusing words are. Take some random sounds and push them out of your mouth in a certain order and at a certain volume, and somehow, other people can understand them.

"Blueberry," I say, and then giggle. It's such a funny word. How do people know what it means? How do they understand that a little blue thing from a vine is a blueberry? How do we all know to use the same word, and who makes that decision?

"There's a couple grand in the mattress in the bedroom," she says. "If I take it, do you want to go to Guymon and board a bus with me?"

Before I can answer, she leans in and kisses me. Her lips are like a cattle prod touching my flesh. When she pulls back, a shadow passes across her eyes. Her nose bends flat on her face, but only for a second, then it's normal again.

"Whoa," I say, breathless. "Did you see that?"

Cassidy grins, letting out a small chuckle. "You're starting to feel it, aren't you? I am too."

"Feel what?"

At first, she says nothing. Then, I remember back at the RV, a million years ago. I was in the bathroom, and she touched me with a wet finger. And I visualize the vials of liquid from Ash's bag, next to the sheets of perforated paper. The vials contain LSD.

"You dosed me," I say.

She takes her head in my hands. "Baby, it's all going to be okay. You have nothing to worry about when you're with me. Ash has the cleanest acid I've ever tasted."

I push her hands away and step off the log, stumbling through the grass. Panic sets in as shadows dance around me. Not like demons or pink elephants, more like the way light bends around a candle when it flickers in a dark room.

The light shifts more harshly, skewing Cassidy's face at a weird angle. It's not right. The image sends a pulse of fear up my spine. I shudder from my head to my toes and have to concentrate to breathe.

"What the hell did you do to me?"

"I told you that you needed to relax. I did this for us. We're going to have a beautiful trip together tonight."

I spin, facing the creek. My body tells me to run to it, to douse myself with water and wash away the impurities.

"Baby," she says, "not that way. If you wander and get

lost, we'll never find you. Please come with me. Let's go back to the RV."

"Why?" I say, hovering on the edge of a dream.

"Because I'm not sure how much I gave you. I think, probably, a lot. You should have a babysitter for the next seven or eight hours, so you don't go crazy on us."

CHAPTER TWENTY-SEVEN

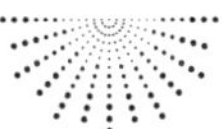

UTAH - FOUR YEARS AGO

Pug and I had made plans to search for Travis in the afternoon, but his injured leg made getting around too difficult. So we rested at the campsite, and I polished off the second fifth of bourbon. After that, I was in no shape to pursue anyone.

He would get up every few minutes and try to put his weight on his leg. He'd make brave faces, grunt, and then he'd sit back down again, panting. After my third or fourth time telling him to give it up, I gave up telling him to give it up.

So we stayed at the campsite, largely in silence. I had no phone service out here, so I played a mobile game until my battery drained down to almost nothing. Waited for the stars to come out, then we retired for the night.

In the morning, Pug wriggled out of the tent. The sound of all the zippers woke me, and I huddled inside my sleeping bag, trying to deny the day. I didn't think he'd be able to move his leg at all because it had turned into a blue and purple mess as the previous evening progressed. But, he made it out of the tent without too much wailing and gnashing of teeth.

He crawled to the flat, grassless area next to the tent to set up the camp stove so we could have our morning oatmeal. I followed him, shuddering the second my body entered the outdoor air. I slipped on every layer I had available and rubbed my hands together until I could feel the sensation in my tingling palms.

"You don't feel weird," he said as he set the tripod stove on the ground, "sleeping next to me in the tent?"

"Swear to God, Pug, I don't give two shits that you're gay."

He nodded and flicked a lighter to start the fire, then poured water from his bottle into the pot.

"Plus," I said, "I kept the Springfield in my sleeping bag. You know, just in case."

He chuckled and then grimaced as he pulled his foot underneath him to sit cross-legged.

"Hurt much?"

"I'll be fine," he said, but his face indicated otherwise.

"Maybe we should get on out of here before it gets any worse."

"No."

"I totally get your dedication, but maybe this is enough. He trapped us in a canyon, and we almost died getting out.

Maybe that's all the sign from above we need to tell us our plan isn't working."

He shook his head, jaw set. "Not until we find Travis."

"And do what? Point guns at him and expect he'll hike out with us and go back to OKC to face Gus? What are we supposed to do if he says no? Are we going to tie him up and drag him through the canyons so random hikers won't see us with him? Because of your leg, I'm not positive we can hike out on the main trails, anyway. If we try going over these cliffs and into the canyons off-trail..."

Pug grasped two packets of dry oatmeal and shook them. He ripped them open and poured the contents into the pot on the stove, into water almost at a boil. "I'm not going to let him get away with what he did."

"What does that mean, exactly?"

He said nothing, but his eyes flicked to the pistol on the ground next to him.

"So you're going to put a bullet in him," I said. "Seriously. Shoot him in the head."

"I don't know. But what do you think Gus will do if we come back empty-handed?"

I shrugged. "He'll be mad, I guess."

"I've been thinking about it a lot. There were things I didn't see before. Things I didn't want to see."

"What does that mean?"

He took the oatmeal off the stove. "I think Gus will be a lot more than mad."

Pug dropped a spoon into the pot and handed the

whole thing to me. When I raised an eyebrow at him, he said, "I'm not hungry."

Then, he walked his Nalgene bottle over to our main water supply. He filled the bottle from one of the two remaining gallon jugs, then he slipped on a jacket. He pointed toward the south. "There's the main trail that way. It leads to an arch named Druid Arch. First, you'll have to hike down into a canyon, then back up, but it doesn't look that bad. Around the arch, there are some good high points to get a look."

"Why are you telling me this?"

He tilted his head back toward the west, where we'd ventured into the slot canyons yesterday. "I'm going that way. We'll split up and meet back here by sunset."

"I don't know if that's a good idea. You can barely walk."

Pug loaded a magazine into his pistol and shoved it in the back of his pants. "We're running out of time, and this is the only way to cover more ground." He tested his leg, grimacing. "We'll meet back here at sunset. And, if you see Travis before I do, shoot him in the chest."

CHAPTER TWENTY-EIGHT

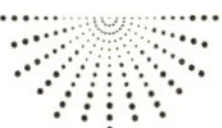

OKLAHOMA - NOW

Boba Fett hasn't spoken to me all day long. I'm not sure where we stand anymore.

I clutch the sides of the sink in the bathroom until I can no longer feel my hands. If I let go, I might fly up and hit the ceiling. My heart screams in my chest and I hardly can hear anything else. *Tha-bump. Tha-bump. Tha-bump.* My sinus passages feel clogged, and my throat numb. It's like a head cold curse bestowed on me by a vengeful gypsy.

How long have I been tripping? Two hours? Four? I'm not sure, but I'm confident I'm at the part referred to as the "peak." Up until this point, the hallucinations have been mild. Shadows skittering, light bending. But now, in this more intense phase of the LSD trip, I'm actually starting to see things. Mainly colors. Like my synapses are misfiring. I look at the toilet, and I know porcelain is white, but it looks green to me. I can't make it stop being green.

Mostly, though, I feel stupid. My brain refuses to work right. Thoughts come, and I try to ride their magic carpet, but I can't grasp the tasseled edge, and I tumble into the void below.

I stare at the inside of the sink as little droplets of blood plummet from the end of my nose and into the basin. *Splot. Splot. Splot.* The droplets flow into pools and mix with the running water to form strings of pink and red as they circle the drain. Fractals and other patterns emerge in the streams. That one looks like a windmill. That one looks like argyle. As the designs swirl, the colors spread and change, the droplets of my vitality turning gray, and orange, then red, then black, palpitating between each different hue.

I look at myself in the mirror, and I don't recognize the face looking back; it appears to be that of a stranger. My pupils have dilated like two black marbles inside slim white rings. The eyebrows look wrong; too thin. The hair is brown and always has been, but it's someone else's hair.

"Micah Reed," I say. "Your name is Micah Reed. Not Michael. It's Micah."

Is that me? How can it be? That's not what I look like. If it's not me, then has someone else infiltrated the bathroom and uncovered a way to enter the mirror and match my every movement?

You're going to die. You're going to die in the prison of this trailer park, and you don't even recognize your own reflection.

I release my grip on the sink and stumble back to the toilet, sitting down with a thud. My limbs and torso have become exceptionally dense, and I don't know if I can rise to my feet ever again. I'm an elephant. Not literally; that would be crazy. I just feel as heavy as one.

I am no longer in control of my body. Trapped inside it. Without warning, my chest lurches and the alien trying to escape my stomach roars as I barf on the floor. Some of it only makes it as far as my throat, and I gulp that back down. Like swallowing fire, I moan from the burning, acidic sensation. It's not an alien, though. Just puke.

A tingle signals the activation of my salivary glands, and rivers of spit fill my mouth. I lean over and let the spit dribble out. *Drip drip drip.* I look down at the vomit on the floor and see mutating fractals again.

Some form of ordered chaos exists in the patterns. Did I create the fractals here, or do they live there already, and I only discovered them?

I can't translate. Can't think straight.

I lower myself from the toilet to the floor, trying to avoid the pulsing, ever-changing mess I've made. I curl up on my side and enjoy the sensation of cold tile supporting my arms and head. The tile pushes against me as I push against it. Action and reaction.

The shoebox is on the floor next to me, and I remove a photograph from the top. Me and Pug in Utah, when my name was Michael McBriar. Before my arrest, before prison. Before we had any idea what was happening around us. Before moving to Denver against my will. Before control-freak Gavin Belmont and all the other insanity in my life.

The person in the picture with his arm around me is dead. I can't reconcile that fact. Don't want to say his name or even think it.

I'll never say his name out loud again.

My hands push my body upright and return the picture to the shoebox. Then I stash the shoebox in the cabinet above the sink, behind the bottles of cleaning liquid. The names on the bottles swirl, like they're floating in front of the screen at a 3D movie. Not actually in space, though. It's an illusion. All of this is a grand illusion.

I stumble out of the bathroom, into the cabin of the RV, and each foot lands heavy as I make my way to the door. Hip bumps against the edge of the couch.

"Sorry, Couch. I didn't see you there."

Out into the night air of the trailer park, it's crisp. Almost cold. The trees sway in the breeze, branches like limbs slashing the air. Doing a dance with themselves, warding off the evil spirits in the air. The grounds seem decidedly barren now. Not a single person out walking. Most of the trailers and RVs are dark, no porch lights illuminating groups sipping beers in folding chairs.

What time is it? How long was I in that bathroom?

My stomach wants to turn again. My head feels too

heavy to sit atop my body. I place my hands on my ears to keep my head from falling off, but it doesn't feel sturdy enough. Squeezing harder seems like a bad idea, though. If I squeeze too tight, I might accidentally twist my head from my neck.

Then, behind me, the shotgun cocks.

I turn to see Poppa Bear, glowering at me. He levels Ash's shotgun at my head. He says nothing at first, but he doesn't have to.

"You piece of shit," he eventually says. Now I realize when Cassidy implied she and Poppa Bear have an *open marriage*, Poppa Bear might not share the same definition. I know he wants to kill me, and I know exactly why. Since a quick and sweaty indiscretion in a teepee in Gloss Mountain State Park, this has been coming. The inevitable confrontation I deserve for the grave mistake I made.

"You just had to put your dick in her, didn't you?"

His words are barely like English. I have to translate each one as it hits my ears, and I struggle to follow along. Like I'm an alien, or he is. I'm not sure which option is better.

I raise my hands. Try to form words, but my mouth feels like it's full of jelly. "I'm sorry. I made a mistake. I feel terrible about this. Trust me. I know it was bad."

"I don't give a shit how you feel."

Where are Cassidy, Dichali, and Ash? How long was I in that bathroom? Has Poppa Bear done something to them? He's holding Ash's shotgun, but the longhaired

Native is nowhere in sight. Poppa Bear has probably killed him. I don't know why I feel so certain about that, but I am. Maybe I was too distracted by the wonder of the fractals in my puke to pay attention.

"Why don't you put the gun down? Let's talk through this."

"You did this to yourself," he says.

Then he wraps his finger around the trigger.

PART III

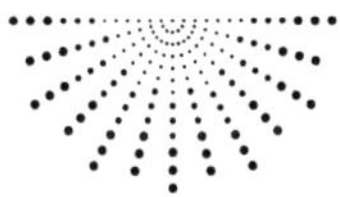

JASPER BELONGS TO EVERYONE

CHAPTER TWENTY-NINE

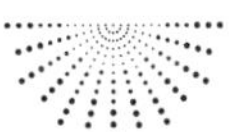

OKLAHOMA - NOW

The shotgun goes off, and for a second, I think I've lost a chunk of my right shoulder. But I quickly realize the shot veered high, and that sensation is the settling of leaves on me from the tree Poppa Bear blasted.

I don't wait around to find out if he'll aim better on the second attempt. I could rush him, but it's dark, I'm extremely (and involuntarily) high on drugs, and in no shape to fight.

Instead, I plot a course into the woods. Dig my feet in. Run. In two seconds, by the time he has the shotgun aimed again, I'm forty or fifty feet away. But the problem is I miscalculated, and I'm sprinting not toward the trees at the edge, I'm headed directly into the trailer park. Along a grass path like a miniature neighborhood street, winding among the rows of rectangular houses.

If he pulls the trigger again, he might hit one of these houses. At best, he might shred someone's window. At worst, he could hit a sleeping resident.

I try to pivot and turn at a ninety-degree angle, but my feet tangle and the ground rushes up to meet me.

My eyes flick up. Poppa Bear, holding the shotgun across his chest, hustles toward me. His tie-dyed shirt is like a kaleidoscope under the moonlight. Eyes are on fire. His teeth like the fangs of a wolf.

"You're dead, you little shit. After everything I did for you, and this is how you pay me back?"

He's closing in on me. I can see the ground reverberate as his sandals pound against the earth.

My hands launch me to my knees, then I'm up on my feet. Running at an angle away from him, toward the woods and the creek I saw earlier. At least, I think it's in that direction. Running, chest heaving, brain like jelly, I'm not sure about anything right now.

But I do make it past him. Running for the trees. It's dark outside. Not sure how late. All of the evening barbecues have been put away. No lovers out for a late night stroll.

No one shouts after us, but I'll bet that shotgun blast woke up a few people, though.

The shotgun roars again, and I stumble out of reflex. But I'm not hit. Or maybe I am, and I can't feel anything yet. Either way, I know I have to run. And watch out for the barbed wire fence. The last thing I want is to tear my flesh and spill my blood in this Godforsaken place.

What will it feel like to be on LSD while injured? With the way my senses are currently heightened, I can't fathom it.

I see the fence up ahead, glinting in the moonlight. But there's no break in it. Nothing but endless, seamless barbed wire in either direction, for as far as I can see.

When I near the fence, I launch my foot on top of it, thinking I'll jump. But it's not springy. My arms pinwheel as I go up and then over the top wire. I topple forward, face full of dirt. Sticks and twigs on the ground scratch my face, like grating cheese.

But I pop back up and settle onto my feet. I can barely breathe, my heart is beating so fast. It's like I'm a race car, revving, circling a track, endlessly making left turn after left after left.

I ignore the thudding in my chest. Ignore the fact that the shadows on everything dance like demons, swirling, making the light unreliable. No idea what is real and what is a figment of my imagination. A few minutes ago, I knew these insane things I was seeing aren't real. Now I don't know.

I ignore the pain on my face and the ache in my back. The tension in my feet as I move. I only think of getting away, reaching somewhere safe.

Five minutes later—or maybe fifty minutes later—I find

myself at the same creek from earlier. I fall to my knees on the muddy banks. Rushing, rushing, water careening along the earth, constrained to a channel in the dirt. The air here is a little cooler. When the world stops, I can hear crickets. But they're incessant. Never ending. Nearly screeching.

When I'm drunk, and something important happens, I can pull it together. I can simulate being sober and make decisions in the moment, almost all the time. But this LSD trip, I can't make it stop. The world swirls around me. My mind is like a blender and thoughts refuse to cooperate. I can't think straight.

When I catch my breath, I sit back on my butt and spread my legs out in front. I take stock of myself. Don't feel any blood on me. Poppa Bear's shotgun didn't connect. I have my wallet in my back pocket, and in a front pocket, I find the knife I appropriated from that redneck yesterday morning, in the parking lot of Shortcakes diner.

Was that really yesterday? Feels like weeks ago.

Then, terror sets in when I realize the things I don't have: my phone. Boba Fett. The shoebox. They're all back in the RV.

Where Poppa Bear is probably waiting for me, shotgun loaded.

CHAPTER THIRTY

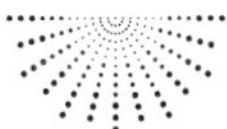

OKLAHOMA - NOW

It's dark all around me. My eyes open, thick and milky at first. I'm panicked because I can't move my arms or legs. It's as if I've been mummified and then set to float in an ocean of air. Somehow, that idea makes sense in my swampy brain.

A tree supports my weight, and I'm sitting, legs out in front of me, hands in my lap. The world is split-screen, half of it is what I can see through my eyes, and the other half is via a camera hovering above me.

I can breathe, but not turn my head. It's like I've gained a thousand pounds and my body is trying to sink into the earth.

The surrounding woods are alive. Breathing, thinking, pulsing with energy. Something brushes against my leg. My eyes flick down to spot a cat's tail. Jasper, the cat from

Stillwater. The one who belonged to the neighborhood. He belongs to everyone.

"You're not here," I say.

Then, a shadow floats a hundred feet in front of me, growing larger. Closer. As the shadow moves in my direction, it takes shape. Human shape. Arms and legs and a torso and a head. As it pulls into focus, my heart rate speeds up. My palms are sweaty, and I can't swallow.

It's my friend. Pug.

He kneels in front of me, that perfect smile spreading across his handsome face.

"Hey, Mikey."

"It's Micah now."

He nods. "I know. You have a new name, and you stopped saying mine."

"Yeah, I did. After prison."

"Why?"

I tilt my head, meeting his eyes. "You know why."

"I need to hear you say it. *You* need to hear you say it. You have to stop keeping these things bottled up, destroying you from the inside out like a flesh-eating bacteria."

"It hurts too much, okay? It's my fault you're dead."

With a sigh, he slips into the grass, on his butt. His hands dig into the surrounding earth, and he draws up a few leaves, which he proceeds to shred. Little bits of decimated leaf flutter in the moonlight, like dust caught in the beam of a flashlight. "It's not your fault, but I know you don't believe it. And I get that you're hurting, Mikey. I'm sorry about that."

"Sometimes, I wonder if you had it the easy way. They're not chasing you anymore."

He frowns. "You're not thinking of…" he lifts a finger to his temple and cocks his thumb to mime pulling a trigger.

I shake my head. "No, I'm not going to kill myself. It's just… my whole situation is swirling the drain right now. And to be honest, life's been rough since you left."

"True. But it was rough for a while before that. We fell into a hole, but the ground kept shifting under our feet. It happened so gradually, we didn't notice. By then, we were in too deep."

He scoots forward in the grass until his knees touch my extended legs. I can't feel it, though. My limbs have all gone numb. I do see blood on his calf from the rock that fell on him in Canyonlands those years ago. Black and blue with bruises.

I couldn't believe he was able to walk after that, let alone hoist a gun and venture off to hunt Travis Pyuen.

"You live in Denver," Pug says, like a question but without elevating his tone at the end of the sentence.

I nod.

"Do you like it?"

I shake my head. "It's not home. I don't have any friends. No family."

"No one?"

"There's my boss at my new job, and he seems like a good guy, but he doesn't drink, plus he's about a hundred years old. We have nothing in common."

Pug stares through me. "In time, he *will* become your friend, though. I know it."

"I don't see how."

"Don't worry about it. Tell me about WitSec."

I shrug. "There's nothing to tell. It's lonely. Isolated. I have a handler named Gavin, and he's a real prick. Always on my case, always acting like I'm going to rush out to rob a bank or blow up a building or something. To him, I'm just another criminal taking advantage of the system and wasting taxpayer money. It's a lot of pressure to live with."

Pug smears some of the blood from his calf on his knees, drawing a smiley face with a bony finger. "That sounds awful."

"What do I do?"

He places his hands on my shins and gives them a squeeze. This, I can feel. "You have to keep going. You can't let them win. No matter what happens, you can't let them win."

A million replies occur to me, but none of them seem fitting. So, I shrug and stare at him.

"Go back to sleep," he says. "Rest up and flush all this acid out of your system. Tomorrow's going to be a big day. If you want to survive it, you need to have your wits about you."

With that, he stands and takes a step back. His features

blur as his body shrinks in size. He's becoming a shadow again. His eyes flicker in the light, two headlamp beacons in darkness. Blasting light at me. Mesmerizing me.

Makes me realize I miss him even more than I thought I did.

"Wait," I say, but he doesn't stop. He skulks back through the woods, dissolving further into mist and darkness.

And then, he's gone.

CHAPTER THIRTY-ONE

OKLAHOMA - NOW

When my eyes open, daylight fills my vision, at first like a yawn. I'm seated against the downed log by the creek, with the folding knife in my hand, blade extended. Legs aching.

I fell asleep? How did that happen? The last thing I remember, I stumbled away from Poppa Bear, trying to take my head off with a shotgun. Wandering out here, then having a crazy vision of a conversation with my best friend.

My mind feels clear, but I can't tell how much of this is real.

I would check the time, but my phone is back in the RV, along with Boba Fett's severed head and my shoebox. The whole damn reason I came here in the first place.

It's Thursday morning. Gavin will be in Denver in twenty-four hours.

The shoebox is at the RV. Among the wolves.

When I stagger to my feet, my back aches. I feel short of breath. I study the knife in my hand. It's not much against shotguns and pistols. But it's all I have, and I'm not going to let them take my shoebox. Not after everything I've been through, after every bump and bruise and moment of panic and peril I've endured over the last few days.

I grip the knife and make my way back toward the trailer park. My feet are heavy like they're wearing cinderblock shoes. But I push forward anyway, gritting my teeth and focusing my bleary eyes on the goal.

In five minutes of slogging through the underbrush and tree limbs, I locate the barbed wire fence. Rusty, dewy, glinting in the morning sun.

And I see the RV in the same spot. It's no longer plugged into the charging station, and that gives me my first bolt of unease. Then, Ash leans out of the open door and closes it behind him.

The RV starts up and backs out of the parking spot. They're leaving.

"No," I say, feeling my stomach sink to the ground. "No, no. You can't go. You have my stuff."

I launch into a sprint, heading for the break in the fence. Feet swishing through grass, the knife in my hand slashing across the air. Queasy stomach seizing as I move. By the time I'm inside the trailer park boundary, the RV is pulling out of the front gate, then turning right. A cloud of dust billowing up on the dirt road around it.

My world closes to a pinhole. They're getting away.

To my right, a lanky guy with a truck is standing near the bed, loading a box into it. He holds a fishing rod in his other hand. He's old, maybe sixties. Shiny bald head with a beard threaded with gray. Wearing a flannel shirt with red and black patches, along with brown coveralls, looking beaten and battered by years of use.

I rush toward him, slipping the knife back into my pocket. "Sir!"

He eyes me, a frown on his face. "Morning. You okay, son?"

"No. Please, I need your help." I point at the front entrance of the trailer park. "The people in the RV that just left stole all my stuff and stranded me here. I have to catch up to them."

He laughs, a small burp of incredulity. "Come again? They did what now?"

"They stole from me. Everything in this world I care about is *on that RV*, and they're going to leave me here and take it from me."

Still, he seems unconvinced. "Are you pulling my leg?"

"We don't have time to argue. Please, I need to borrow your truck."

"That ain't gonna happen, son."

For a second, I consider the knife in my pocket. Would be easy to whip it out and demand his keys. But, I don't want to be that person who will use power to get whatever he wants. "Then drive me. They left ten seconds ago, so I'm sure we can catch up. Please, I'm begging you. I can't let them get away."

He scratches the top of his head a few times, then he nods. "Alright, then. Hop in."

I scramble over to the passenger side as he drops his fishing pole in the bed, then he waddles to the driver's side. Inside the truck, he starts it up. The engine churns, and I'm tapping my foot, panicked. An ancient knob-based radio flicks on to some AM station. A preacher giving a sermon over the muted sounds of a pipe organ. I hear the words *God* and *Hallelujah* and *Jesus* and *Repent* before I jab out a finger and turn it off. My driver gives me a look as he puts the truck in gear, but doesn't turn the radio back on.

As he turns his truck around to face the entrance, he removes a phone from his breast pocket and tries to pass it to me.

"What's that for?" I ask.

"So you can call the police. If they stole from you, I assume you aim to file charges on them, right?"

I wave him off. There are plenty of reasons for me to fear interaction with the police. If I were even interested in explaining the whole sordid situation to this guy, I wouldn't even know where to start. "No charges. I just want my stuff back."

"Suit yourself."

We pull out of the parking lot, and I point to the right. The old man doesn't quite display the level of urgency I'm seeking. I'm bouncing in the seat, and he's humming a little tune under his breath as his truck struggles to accelerate.

"You okay?" he says.

"No, I'm not. These people are trying to strand me here after stealing the only thing in the world that matters to me. I'm pretty far from okay."

He doesn't seem to know what to say to that, so he closes his mouth and points his eyes forward. In another few thousand feet, the road ends in a T-junction.

I look left and look right. Don't see anything. But, if I remember correctly, the RV had been low on gas yesterday when we arrived at the trailer park. "Is there a gas station near here?"

He points right. "There's a truck stop near four-twelve, about a half mile over that way."

"Please, take me there."

He tilts his head in each direction, checking for traffic, but then a car comes up behind us. Gives a gentle honk. He checks the rearview and lifts a hand to the car behind us, then turns right.

In a half mile, I see a giant hamburger at the top of a towering pole. The sign below it reads *Truck Stop*, no name. And there, in the parking lot, is the RV. I witness Dichali, Ash, Poppa Bear, and Cassidy exiting the vehicle, walking toward the front door of the building. They must be stopping for breakfast.

Maybe they've already filled the gas tank or maybe not, but this is the best chance I have.

"There!" I say, a little too loud. The old man flinches. "Sorry. It's them, in that RV right there. You can drop me off at the edge of the parking lot."

"Son, are you sure you don't want to call the law? Are these the same people that was shooting off guns in the trailer park last night?"

I look him in the eye, and he wavers back and forth between watching me and watching the road. "No. And please don't call the cops after you drop me off. I need to handle this on my own. Anything you do to help is only going to end up hurting. Trust me."

"Okay, then, if that's how you want to play it."

He pulls into the lot and circles back, toward the edge of the lot. I shake his hand and exit the vehicle without a word. Slip the knife from my pocket. I wait until his truck leaves me before I extend the blade. Holding. I'm not sure exactly what I plan to do with it, but I know one thing for sure.

I'm getting my damn shoebox back.

Staying low, I creep across the lot, keeping the RV between me and the truck stop, so I'm shielded. When I'm near the vehicle, I creep toward the front. Spy a look inside the truck stop. Through the window, I see them.

Dichali and Poppa Bear are standing over Cassidy, glowering. Her shoulders are slumped, her face down.

I have a hard time feeling sorry for her, though. She lied to me and then dosed me with LSD against my will. Even if I didn't have a shotgun-wielding, crazed hippie after me, I still would not have wanted the gift of a ten-hour acid trip.

They're standing near the air fresheners in the convenience store section of the truck stop. Across from a Subway restaurant. That should buy me a few minutes if they sit down to eat.

I slide the knife into the lock on the side door and apply pressure. It's harder to pick a lock with a knife as opposed to proper tools, but I know how to do this. The trick is to wiggle the tip of the blade in as deep as possible, and then press up while rotating clockwise. Mechanical locks only. This is an older RV, and the locks don't look electric.

I give it a test turn to the right and the door swings open. It actually wasn't even locked. I jump inside and close the door behind me. The keys to the RV are sitting on the dash, out in the open for all to see. Seems insane, with all the guns and drugs stashed around the cabin.

I've got no time to worry about that now. First, my phone. It's sitting on the table in the kitchen. I snatch it and shove it in my pocket. Then, Boba Fett. I open the bathroom door, and he's sitting in the soap tray. He goes in my other pocket.

I'm almost whole again. Only one more thing.

Last place I remember seeing the shoebox was on the floor in the bathroom. But it's not here now.

"Think, Micah. Did you put it somewhere?"

I leave the bathroom as my eyes flick over every available surface, surrounded by cabinets and drawers. I open a few in the kitchen. Piles of forks and spoons, spatulas, an egg beater, but no shoebox.

"Shit!"

I move to the front of the cabin, to the seats. There's nothing here, either.

The truck stop front door opens, and Poppa Bear struts outside. A second later, Dichali and Cassidy join him. Headed back toward the RV.

"No." What are they doing? Then, I note the bags of chips and sodas in their hands. Instead of sitting down to eat a meal, they've opted for road snacks. They'll be here in twenty seconds.

But where is Ash? I could have sworn I saw him exiting the RV with the rest of them.

It doesn't matter. They're inbound, and I still haven't found the shoebox. Think, Micah, think. Running out of time.

Only one option appears valid. The keys are on the dash. If the shoebox is in the RV, I can retrieve it later.

I snatch the keys and slide into the captain's chair. Start up the monstrosity and watch Poppa Bear meet my eyes. His mouth drops open, and he lets his bottle of

Mountain Dew slip from his fingers and bounce on the ground.

I give him a little grin as I put it in gear and turn the wheel. The metal beast is large, heavy, and hard to turn.

The RV angles as I push the gas, headed for the exit. Poppa Bear and Dichali break out into a run. Cassidy is standing there in the parking lot, her eyes wide.

As I pull toward the exit and roll out into the street, I think again of Ash. Where did he go? Still in the bathroom?

But, I don't have to wait long to get the answer to that question. As I floor the gas and the RV kicks into gear, he leaps out of the back bedroom, a Smith & Wesson M&P .40 in his hand.

CHAPTER THIRTY-TWO

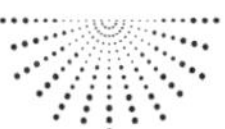

UTAH - FOUR YEARS AGO

With my gun, water, Boba Fett, binoculars, and a park map in a small daypack, I set off to the south across Chesler park. Shuffling along the thin dirt trails snaking through the grass of this wide-open space ringed by massive rock spires.

The lack of people hadn't bothered me the way I expected it would. The lack of animals was a pleasant surprise, though. I'd prepared myself for scorpions, tarantulas, wolves, lions, tigers, and bears. So far though, none of those creatures had made any appearances.

Pug had wandered back toward the slot canyons an hour before. I'd been no fan of splitting up, but Pug had seemed obsessed. In all the years I'd known him, he'd always been the voice of reason. The one to warn me about the dangers of doing whatever stupid thing I'd intended to do.

In school, when I'd had the idea to hood surf behind the abandoned grocery store at 81st and Yale in Tulsa, he'd come up with the idea of using bungee cords to secure our feet to the hood. I would have never thought of that. He probably saved my life that night.

This new, reckless Pug seemed so foreign to me. Was he rattled about coming out, maybe? Many of our associates, particularly the ones from Mexico, said unkind things about gay people. He could have feared for his job security. Or maybe he was worried about something worse than losing his job… after what we'd learned about Gus and his violent side, I didn't know what to think anymore. I wasn't sure if either of us valued our job security any longer. It seemed like a good time to find a new line of work, actually.

First, though, we had to see this through. Not that I cared about Travis Pyuen and punishing him for stealing from our boss. But I did care about backing up Pug and making sure he didn't die out here with his injured leg. Travis had proved he was cunning and ruthless. Not someone to underestimate.

If we didn't find him first, good chance he would come find us.

At the edge of Chesler, a wooden sign pointed toward Elephant Canyon and Druid Arch. The trail quickly turned from a grassy path into sandy washes and slick rock walls snaking into a gradually rising elevation. Giant sheets of pale pink boulders and sparse trees spaced out throughout the crunchy surface of dried-up riverbeds.

By the time the sun had risen halfway up the sky, I had to shed my outer layers. Felt my skin cooking, even though it couldn't have been more than fifty degrees outside. Beads of sweat on my forehead and down my back. As I strayed further and further away from the campsite, I thought about the water attached to my belt. I had two one-liter bottles, which was about half of the water we had left. Total. That meant no matter what, we had no choice but to hike out tomorrow. Or, maybe even tonight, depending on how the day went. The only water I'd seen out here were puddles of green, stagnant liquid with mosquitoes buzzing around. I didn't trust iodine tablets to make that water safe for human consumption.

Maybe that's why Pug had insisted we split up. The clock was running out to find and deal with Travis. He knew we had only today to accomplish our task, or we run back to Gus empty-handed. And, we now both knew how mad Gus could become when he didn't get what he wanted.

Or did we? Did we have any actual idea how mad he could get?

At the crest of the next rock hill, the path opened up to a long canyon with a series of bends down below. The rock formations on either side of the canyon weaved back and forth, making the canyon snake through them. Down there, it looked like hours of back-and-forth navigation to reach the other side. As beautiful as it was intimidating.

I could see a series of small rock cairns leading me down into the canyon. After pulling Boba Fett from my pocket, I held him out. "Look at this, Boba. Nice view, right?"

It's nice, Mike. Going to be a long way down, though.

"True, but I don't see that I have a choice. Pug is expecting me to find this Druid Arch, so that's where I'm headed."

Sounds good. I'm along for the ride, either way, so you won't hear any complaints from me. Just be careful.

"That word doesn't really register for me."

I know, I know. But try not to die out here.

I returned Boba to my pocket and set off down the rock, contemplating what it meant to be careful. Thinking about slipping, falling and breaking my ankle, being unable to hike back out. I'd seen exactly one other person this morning, a woman with a backpack, hiking along a ridge parallel to me. She'd raised a hand in a wave, then I'd done the same, and the transaction had ended. No other humans had crossed my field of view in hours.

How long could I survive out here, all by myself, rationing out the little water I had?

Small ridges made steps as I descended into the canyon. At the bottom, I found a rocky and dry creek bed twisting back and forth. I followed this for an hour, occasionally stopping to sip my water. Had to be careful. I wasn't sure how far I'd come, but the route back could take me all day, depending on how deep in this canyon I had to venture to find the arch.

I wasn't even sure how far I was supposed to go. The plan was to ascend to a high point past the arch and then scout for Travis. Seemed like an unlikely proposition, because it wasn't as if there was a single mountaintop high point to see the whole park. Everything below was a series of cliffs and canyons, many of them slim slots where the highest point was ground level. You could hide deep down in one of those things forever and not be visible from above.

When I realized that, I paused and put my hands on my hips. How the hell did I expect to locate anything out here? With only one day left to accomplish finding the needle in the haystack?

Didn't matter. I had to press on.

After another half hour, Elephant Canyon opened up to a circular area, and I discovered something that could only be Druid Arch. Massive rock shooting up from the earth, like a large "A" dropped onto the land by the gods above. When I first saw it, I had to pause for a few moments to gawk before I could continue. Breathtaking.

By this time, the sun was beginning its slow descent across the sky, and I could see the high point Pug had referred to. Past the arch, a trail led up to the top of the canyon. Maybe three or four hundred feet of elevation above sea level.

I set off around the arch, following a series of little canyons and ridges that led in a wide arc around Druid Arch. The slim path grew steeper and steeper until I had a hundred foot drop on my right and a sheer rock wall on my left. At my feet, a twenty-inch path cutting across the rock. I tried not to think about it or look down. Focused on setting each foot down solidly before picking up the next.

When the climb started to ascend even steeper, I held my hands out. "Okay, you can do this."

Up ahead, the path cut between two rocks. Barely wide enough for me to fit through. I lowered my hips for better balance and geared up to squeeze into the slim space between them.

Something caught when I tried to break through to the other side. The belt on my pants tugged. I felt my pants slipping, exposing my butt crack. When I tried to turn and fix it, something scraped against my hip. I yelped and pulled back, toward the trail I'd come from.

And then I felt the belt detach. Heard plastic thudding on the rock as I suddenly grew lighter. When I turned to investigate the sound, I watched my two water bottles sailing off the rock wall and descending into the canyon below. Bouncing, spinning, twisting all the way down. They crashed to the bottom, cracking into dozens of pieces, leaving little puddles of water.

Gone.

Now, I was miles away from my campsite, with no water.

CHAPTER THIRTY-THREE

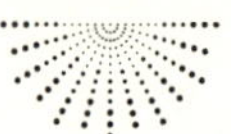

OKLAHOMA - NOW

I'm on the road, navigating this house with wheels, trying not to run it off into the ditch. But, the immediate problem is the scowling, long-haired Native American man with the pistol, stomping through the back of the RV on a collision course with me. Long, luxurious hair swinging from side to side with each stomp of his foot.

His pistol is raised, pointed at my head. He has one eye closed, the other staring down the sights. Via his gritted teeth, I can feel the rage emanating from him like radio waves.

"Pull over," he says.

"I can't do that."

His finger wraps around the trigger. "Do it now. Pull this vehicle over to the side of the road, or I'm going to shoot you in the back of the head."

"If you shoot me, this thing is going off the road, and you're not wearing a seatbelt. We'll both die in very not-nice ways."

"That won't be your problem when you're dead," he says.

He's standing five feet behind my chair, legs spread shoulder-width, knees slightly bent. It's not the most secure stance. He's not braced against anything. His anger has clouded his judgment, and that's maybe the only advantage I have right now.

An impulse comes over me. I jerk the wheel to the right, and he topples. The gun goes flying from his hand as his body ripples in a wave like he's overcome with the holy spirit.

But, what I don't anticipate is how this behemoth traveling vehicle reacts to a quick twist of the wheel. The front lurches right, but then the *back* of the RV pivots left, and for a second, it feels like the middle of the RV has twisted like a corkscrew. My captain's chair swivels and I rock back and forth. Instinct makes me shove the wheel back in the other direction before it goes too far out of control.

Ash stumbles back a step and smacks against the counter with the sink. He doubles over and then stumbles into the couch. His pistol slides away from him, toward the back of the RV.

I'm watching all this out of the corner of my eye, but I'm mostly focused on not crashing the RV. It's my first time driving one. I'm wiggling the steering wheel, trying with all my power not to overcompensate and swing the wheel too far in either direction. It's a challenge because the road is a little bumpy, so the wheel wants to shimmy in my hands like a wet dog trying to flee bath time.

Ash stands from the couch and grabs hold of the table behind it. He bears down, panting. Feet spread wide now, arms out to balance himself.

"Pull over now, or I'm going to make you suffer, you little ant."

And right then, I consider a full inventory of my plan and everything I need to do. Ideally, I'd pull over and search the RV for the shoebox. Once I have that, there's no reason for me to stick around any longer, or to have anything to do with these people. I'd take my possessions and be free of them forever, leaving the next step as something to figure out later.

But, what am I supposed to do with Ash on board? If I pull over, I'm dead, but it's not as if I can keep driving forever. And while both of my hands are occupied, he has a distinct advantage. If he finds his gun, which appears to be sliding around on the floor behind us, he can shoot me at any time.

I'm flying blind here without an endgame.

He lurches from the table to the counter, grasping the edge of it. He's wise to my swerve game now, because he's clinging to a series of stable objects so I can't do that again. Not sure if I would even attempt that move now. Jerk the wheel too hard, and this hurtling rectangle might shake itself to pieces.

Ash looks around for the gun, but it's skittered somewhere out of sight. Then, he digs a hand into his pocket and whips out a straight razor. He flicks it open with one hand and holds it up to eye level. It's silvery and shining under the sunlight pouring in through the windows.

"I'm going to cut your eyes out and feed them to you before you die."

He lands one foot closer, then the other. Three steps behind me. The razor in his hands shakes from the intensity of his grip.

I'm driving and in no position to defend myself. If I take my hands off this wheel, the RV will crash. If I don't defend myself, he can kill me with one swipe of that blade. Neither of those seems like a good outcome.

But, I have to pick one. Indecision is no longer an option.

To my left is an open field, rows of wheat like rippling ocean waves. To my right is a dense thicket of trees, seemingly endless.

I look down to confirm that my seatbelt is buckled.

There's really only one avenue left.

When he lifts his leg to take another step, I wrench the wheel to the right with all my power. The RV swerves, but only for a second. In a flash, it's traveling sideways. Tilting. Tires scream underneath the vehicle.

Then, the world banks. Folds on itself. Gravity pulls me, shifting me to one side of the chair. The sideways-traveling RV bends in the middle of the road. It's leaning, with the driver window fast approaching the ground. Coming up to meet me, a blur of pavement and the dotted white highway divider. My stomach lurches up into my throat as my body strains against the limits of the seatbelt holding me in place.

As the RV tilts, I see Ash in my peripheral. He's floating in the air, hands up, legs out, as if we're in zero gravity. His hair spreads out in all directions like Medusa's snakes.

I'm sideways. The seatbelt is the only thing keeping me from tumbling out into space with him.

Then the world shakes as the driver's side wall becomes the floor. That side of the RV connects with something hard and impenetrable. My body thrashes around, my head snapping back and forth. The seatbelt slashes across the flesh of my neck. Burning.

My ears fill with the sound of grinding metal and glass. The window to my left explodes and my eyes shut against the barrage of shrapnel pelting the inside of the cabin. I feel a dozen scrapes across my face.

The metal screams, making my ears pulse. My hands are locked on the wheel, gripping it so hard I think I'm going to rip it off. The RV is skidding and sliding, but no longer careening through the air.

And then it slows.

I open my eyes, now completely sideways. Hanging from the captain's chair. The passenger side is above me.

Behind me, dishes and glasses from the kitchen crash to the floor, which used to be the left side of the vehicle.

But I don't know where Ash is. I can't hear him, but my ears are ringing. The RV is still scooting forward, still shifting and crunching. All the grinding and screeching and sliding slows and then stops. The inertia of the moving vehicle makes it heave forward one last time, and then it leans in the other direction. It stalls, exhausted.

The giant traveling box has stopped.

I jab at the seatbelt release button, but my bodyweight has put too much tension on it. I can't press the button inward to unclasp my belt.

But my hands are free. I reach into a pocket and withdraw my folding blade. Have to hurry. The seatbelt is cutting off the circulation to my neck, and I'm starting to grow woozy. Can't inhale.

I slash the blade against the seatbelt, near my torso. After a couple of flicks, the fabric splits, and I fall. The upper part of the belt catches me under the armpit, twisting me in place. My legs smack against the driver side window. Glass shifts underneath me. But at least I can breathe now. I heave in a deep lungful as my vision swims with stars.

Have to hurry. Any second now, Ash will come leaping over this chair, attacking me with the straight razor. I don't know if I can lift this blade again to defend myself.

When I free my arm from the seatbelt, it takes me a couple moments to return to normal breathing and regain my bearings. The whole world is sideways. It's disorienting.

But, when I can see again, Ash is in front of me. Not primed to attack. He's bent backward over the kitchen counter, limp, limbs hanging down on either side. His eyes are blank, and his mouth opens and closes, like a fish trying to suck in oxygen.

I vault over the chair, knife out. He doesn't turn to face me. Eyes up, motionless. His long hair unmoving, pointed down.

I step over the side door, with the couch above my head. Ashkii's eyes are full of panic. His breaths come fast and ragged, and then they slow. His face freezes and his eyes go cold.

Must have broken his back falling on the counter.

I wait a moment longer. He stops breathing.

My attacker is dead, but the owner of this RV is still out there, back at the truck stop a mile or two down the road. And now, the police are surely en route. Only a matter of minutes before this RV will be surrounded by people with guns. I'm a prisoner inside this box.

What the hell am I supposed to do?

CHAPTER THIRTY-FOUR

OKLAHOMA - NOW

Ash is dead in front of me, or, at least, he looks dead. When my ears stop ringing, I wade through a sea of broken and torn things, intending to place a finger on the side of his neck. The last thing I want is him bursting to life and slashing me with his straight razor, which he's still gripping in his lifeless hand.

My hand hesitates, hovering a few inches away from his flesh. What if he snaps awake? I clear my throat and remind myself of the time crunch. My fingers feel no beating pulse. His eyes are open, staring blankly into space. He's dead.

That's one problem solved, but it won't be enough to ensure I live out the day. There's still the matter of me being trapped, halfway across the country, and probably soon having to deal with a fair amount of legal scrutiny.

My foot crunches glass, and my eyes travel downward. And there, I notice the strangest thing: a vast collection of twenty dollar bills. They're everywhere. Hundreds of them, some still floating, falling onto the floor.

There's a mattress in the hall, leaning against the bathroom door. And I remember Cassidy telling me about the cash hidden in the bed. The mattress is *above* me, and there's a hole in the bottom of it, pregnant with illicit money. A few more bills slip out of the hole, fluttering in the air as they cascade toward me.

A thousand bucks is floating inside this RV, waiting for me to scoop it up. Begging for me to take it. Sitting everywhere on top of a bed of broken glass and plastic.

I snatch as many bills as I can get my hands on. Fifty, sixty, seventy; I'm not sure how many. Enough to make my back pocket bulge as I shove the bills inside. There's another problem solved, but it's still not good enough. I'm not done yet. I need the shoebox. Without that one item, all of this has been for nothing.

I'm going to get what I came for, even if it kills me.

I stagger along the left wall of the RV, which is now the floor. The kitchen is beneath me, and I place hesitant steps over the oven. I have to test my foot on top of the dishwasher to make sure I won't break the door and twist my ankle.

The dining table and chairs bolted to the wall are now above me. It's like being inside some bizarre art installation. My tired brain keeps orienting it ninety degrees so I can make sense of what I'm doing.

"Come on, universe, give me a damn break, here."

Then, I see it. Underneath the mattress, on top of the bathroom door. My shoebox. The top is off, and a couple of the pictures are sitting on the door next to it. Plus the business card with the wolf logo and one of the thumb drives my friend gave me before he died.

It's all there, scattered among the broken plates and glasses.

I shuffle through the debris and scoop everything back into the box, then cradle it under my arm. When I turn, I note Ash's pistol near the front of the RV, sitting in a pile of dirty laundry. A sundress, Cassidy's. As mad as I am at her for dosing me with LSD against my will, I still hope she's okay. I know she doesn't want to be stuck with these people, either.

I creep over to the pistol and pick it up, shaking it to free loose pieces of glass from the top. Crinkle and crunch of stray bits falling to the floor.

Check the magazine. It's loaded.

Now, how to get out of here? The side door is above me, ten feet in the air. I could maybe stand on top of the couch to reach it, but it would be a difficult stretch. Even if I can get my hands on it, I'll have to toss the shoebox up while my feet dangle in the air, and I don't want the contents to splatter everywhere. Might not have time to gather it all up again. Only now do I realize how much it would have helped me if I'd sealed it with some duct tape. A little late for that now, though.

I don't hear sirens outside yet, but they'll be coming. Soon. There's no doubt about that. Even if some random farmer didn't see or hear the crash, someone else will come along this highway and call them.

Exiting via the passenger door is a better bet than from the side. I can climb from the driver's chair to passenger chair, which will place me only a couple feet below that door to the side/top of the RV.

Shaky limbs scramble over the couch and push me on top of the driver's captain chair as I shove the pistol in the back of my jeans, then I reach up and wrap one arm around the far side of the passenger seat. I lift myself, bracing my feet against the dashboard. Bits of glass slide off the passenger seat, slicing across my face. Taste some blood on my lip. My arms shake, holding on for dear life. I have barely anything left in me to give to my escape.

I transition my feet over to the passenger chair, clinging to it. It's like trying to hold on to a recliner chair from the side while it hovers in midair. Terribly awkward. I dig my feet into the interior left side of the chair, which is now below me. Now I can extend my legs, with something solid beneath my feet. I push higher and grasp the door handle. Instinct tells me to swing it *out,* but it needs to go up instead. All the way up and then over, so it won't slam shut again. It's heavy. I bear down with my feet, so I can stand up and throw a shoulder against the door. Below me, the passenger seat creaks. It's sinking, bending against the pressure of my full weight. You're not supposed to stand on the side of a chair.

With one final heave, I open the door, swinging it up and out. I have to grab it, so it doesn't close again on top of me. Then, I hoist the shoebox up, onto the exterior of the vehicle. Place both my hands on the edges and lift myself out of the RV. I'm sitting on the side of the vehicle, facing a blue sky. The front right tire is directly beside me. Smells like burnt rubber.

And then, across the field, a red Ford truck races into view. Swerving through the grass, barreling toward the wrecked RV.

The truck stops a hundred feet away. It parks and the doors fly open. Dichali and Poppa Bear stumble out, with Cassidy being dragged by the arm behind them.

I can read the venom in Poppa Bear's eyes and see his yellow teeth bared. And he's headed right for me.

CHAPTER THIRTY-FIVE

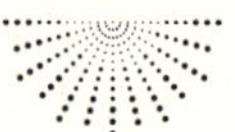

UTAH - FOUR YEARS AGO

I had a decision to make: without water, I wasn't going to last out here overnight. The sun was setting. The hike back to our campsite would take maybe three or four hours, or I could press on toward the high point and complete the task I'd set out to do.

Spotting Travis from an elevated position still seemed like a pipe dream, but it was all I had left.

My water bottles were in pieces at the bottom of this hiking trail. Plastic broken, the water consumed by the thirsty dirt. My mouth was already dry. Whether I scouted ahead or turned back to the campsite, I'd be out of water for the duration, either way.

I had a headlamp in the small daypack I'd brought with me, plus the light on my phone. And while the idea of going back to the campsite tempted me, I still had a job to do. Somewhere out here, Pug was on his own, hunting for

Travis, so I had to keep up my end of the bargain. Especially since I would only need about ten more minutes of hiking to reach the high point past the arch.

I donned the headlamp and continued up the trail, keeping my eyes down to be sure of the ground in front of me. Some patches were pure slick rock, others were bits of sand and orange scree spread out across the path.

My legs burned. Back ached. Dry throat made swallowing a challenge.

In a few minutes, I crested the top of the trail, out onto a flat plateau of vast rock. Cairns led off to continue the trail, but I didn't need to go any further. The sun had set, but I could still see in every direction. The faint light of pre-dark showed me a wide open space, stretching for dozens or hundreds of miles in every direction.

"Holy shit," I said. Standing there, in the fading light of the middle of a vast desert, I felt tiny. Insignificant. You don't get views like this in Oklahoma. Or, at least, I'd never seen one.

I killed my headlamp light and let my eyes adjust to the fading twilight. Turned in circles, squinting to see. And then, out of the corner of my eye, the dim light bent and wavered in one particular spot. Something unnatural. I turned my head toward it and leaned forward to find what looked like a shadow snaking up through the air.

I took a few steps toward it and realized it was *smoke* coming down out of the canyon to the west. Nowhere near the campsite Pug and I had made.

A backpacker, out on his own?

After crossing to that side of the plateau, I lifted the binoculars to my face. Took a few seconds to adjust to the dusk. The line of smoke traced down to a slot canyon below. When my eyes came to the fire, the brightness of it made me wince and pull my head away from the binoculars. I blinked a few times and then resumed, letting my eyes take it in a little more gradually this time.

And when I could locate the fire, I spotted Travis sitting next to it, his wide frame hulking as he poked at it with a stick. A few embers danced in the air above the fire.

And next to the fire was Pug. Except, he wasn't sitting, he was on his side, duct tape over his mouth and hands, his legs bound with rope.

My heart thudded. Travis had Pug, bound and gagged. I should have known he was in no shape to rush off in pursuit.

This was all my fault. I'd let Pug walk into some sort of trap.

The next thought came suddenly: Travis wanted me to find them. Wanted to have it out, right there in the slot canyon. That had to be why he'd lit a fire; he knew I would find it when I searched for Pug. I was likely about to encounter the same trap that had snared my best friend.

My hands shook, and I had trouble focusing through the binoculars. Took me a few seconds to breathe and calm down enough to think. I had a feeling I was about to walk into something I couldn't walk out of, but I didn't know what other choice I had.

There were two entrances to the slot canyon where Travis was. One in front and one behind. The cliff walls on either side were too steep for me to use. As I watched him by the fire, I noted he never turned around. Always looking in one direction.

Option one, or option two? Travis would have to be prepared for both. He would probably assume I'd approach from behind, and he would use a mirror or something to track me. Then, I would get too close, and he'd lift the pistol at Pug's head. Then, I'd be at his mercy, and I lose all of my leverage. He'd make me drop my gun, and then it's only two quick pulls of the trigger to send us both into the dirt.

I had to manufacture an element of surprise. So, I would go straight in. Stick to the wall, hide in the shadows, and rush him. The slot looked curvy enough that I could get pretty close before he'd see me.

I'd put a bullet in his head before he could do anything about it.

My hand curled back to the Springfield 1911 pistol, sticking out of my back belt loop. In the course of working for Gus and his people in Oklahoma City, I'd waved the pistol around lots of times. I'd broken the teeth of a few assholes by smacking them in the mouth with the barrel. I'd even fired some warning shots. But never had I killed anyone before. Never shot a man in the head, or the chest, or anywhere. Now, I knew I had to. If it came down to Pug's life or this man's, I would do what I needed to do.

I took off my headlamp and pointed it at the ground, so I could still see my feet, but the light wouldn't bounce all over the place. I had to retrace my steps on the trail back toward the arch, then I found a way into the slot canyon, lower in the canyon valley. There didn't seem to be an official trail down there, but after hunting around, I noted a section of the rock wall I could scramble down. Assuming it would hold.

Carefully, I went hand over foot down the rocks, tapping my foot on each one below before letting my weight fall on it. Wondered if this was technically rock climbing.

A couple minutes later, I found myself at the bottom of the side canyon where I figured the light had come from. But, I couldn't be sure. I would have to explore.

Crunchy rocks shifted under my feet. The canyon had enough bends in it that I couldn't see Travis from here, at first. After a couple minutes of slow tramping through a dry river gulch, I could see that smoke sticking out from the top of the canyon, a hundred feet above my head.

This was it, just up ahead.

Headlamp off, gun out. Finger on the trigger.

I couldn't see much of anything since the moon was a sliver, and the stars weren't fully out yet. Just the dim echo of dusk light filtering down into this rocky terrain.

I used my gun as a navigator, holding it out in front

and letting it be the guide. I wanted to shuffle my feet for safety, but I worried that might make too much noise. Instead, I lifted each foot and let it drift out in front of me before placing it, trying to sense changes in elevation. If I took a tumble over a rock and sprained my ankle, that would be the end of the line.

As I curved through the bends in the slot canyon, the light from Travis' fire provided a little illumination. Growing brighter with each step. I could now see it at the edge of the next bend.

I was close. Raised my gun. Edged up to the cliff wall. Deep breath in, then pushed it out, trying to keep my heart rate normal. Wasn't working. My palms were sweaty, my mouth dry, my knees weak. If ever there was a time to be confident and decisive, this was it. I seemed to be failing on all counts.

After one more deep breath, I jumped around the last bend. Travis looked up. I noted an object in his hand. Not a gun, but a piece of rope.

He jerked the rope, and something clicked. Before I had time to react, a stick to the right of me moved, and a cluster of rocks tumbled from a ledge. Dozens or hundreds of them, some as large as softballs, pelting me. One knocked the gun from my hand, and a basketball-sized rock smacked me in the knee. Another pelted the side of my head. The accumulation of blows sent me to the ground within a second of my arrival.

The last of the rocks fell, and I was half covered in them. Knee throbbed, head pounding.

I panicked, searching around for the gun. Rocks trickled away from me like water cascading in a shower. I tried to lift myself out of the rocks, but couldn't stretch my legs to get them under me.

"Stop," Travis said. I looked up to find him standing next to the fire, holding pistols in each of his hands. One of them was Pug's.

"If you start digging through that pile of rocks for your gun, I'll shoot your friend here first, then I'll shoot you next. Got it?"

CHAPTER THIRTY-SIX

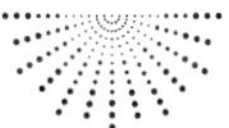

OKLAHOMA - NOW

As Poppa Bear and Dichali race across the field toward me, dragging Cassidy behind them, I snatch the shoebox, slide over the tire, and land on the ground. Gunshots ping against the side of the RV. Some bounce away, ricocheting off the two-lane highway. Some punch through, bouncing around inside the beached whale of a vehicle.

"You son of a bitch!" Poppa Bear says. "You wrecked my ride!"

I sprint around the front of the RV, hiding by the passenger side. I'm not sure if bullets will penetrate this window, but they might. Probably, they will. I can't stay here. But, the woods are more than a hundred feet to my left, so I'm not sure if it's a good idea to bolt in that direction yet.

Poppa Bear and Dichali creep up to the opposite edge

of the RV. They each fire a few times toward me, but I pull my body out of view. We're all stuck on opposite sides of this rectangle. Not much we can do besides circle each other.

Unless they get smart and split up, each of them going in a different direction. Maybe I can take them on one-by-one that way, or maybe they surround me, and I'll be overwhelmed. Whatever happens, this dance won't last long.

I sneak over to the other side of the RV. There's a luggage rack running along the side facing me, so I set the shoebox down and grab hold of it. I scale it like a storm drain on the side of the building. When I get to the top, I crawl across the RV, closer to their position. They're still shooting at where they think I am.

After a few seconds, they're within sight. The side/roof of the RV bends and creaks a little as I crawl across it, so I'm careful to move slowly. Don't want to give away my position.

Poppa Bear and Dichali are leaning around the edge of the back of the RV. Cassidy standing behind them, hands over her ears. She's shuddering, quaking. Tears running down her cheeks. And I note she now has a black eye to compliment the bruises on her arms.

I move from prone to a knee and take aim. Any man who would hit a woman needs to learn a lesson, and I'm not leaving here today until I feel like Poppa Bear has been schooled.

Cassidy looks up and sees me. Her mouth drops open. I

close one eye, trying to line up the sight. It's hard up here, from this elevated position. My heart is racing, and I have trouble focusing. Need a few more seconds.

But she acts first. She grabs something from Dichali's back pocket. A knife. Without any warning, she jabs it into his shoulder blade. Probably thinks she's helping me, but she's muddied up my line of sight, and now it's all chaos on the ground below.

Dichali screams and whirls on her. One hand digging at the knife jutting from his back, the other trying to swipe at her.

I have no choice. She's put herself in direct danger.

I aim and fire, sending one bullet into Dichali's back. Circle of red widening on his white shirt. He staggers, and I shoot him again, and this one drops him. Flat on his face in the middle of the road.

A bullet whizzes past my left ear, so I duck. Didn't see where it came from. I was sloppy, not paying attention.

"I see you up there," Poppa Bear says. "Get the fuck off my RV."

I scoot a few feet to my right and jump up, weapon raised. But now, Poppa Bear has one arm around Cassidy, using her as a human shield. The other hand holding the gun, extended out toward me.

"It's over," Poppa Bear says. "Come down and let's talk about this. You might think I won't kill my old lady, but you don't know me very well."

Gun raised, I move a few feet back so he can't shoot me

while I'm descending. I scamper down the front tire again, keeping my pistol raised and pointed at him all the while.

"Put your gun down," he says as I square up against him, thirty feet away.

"I don't think so. This is the only thing keeping you from killing her."

She whimpers when my words hit her ears. "Micah, I'm so sorry. Please know that I'm sorry."

Poppa Bear growls. "Shut your damn mouth, woman."

In the distance, the whine of sirens fades in. Not far away, maybe a mile or two. But it grows louder each second. Cops, or an ambulance, or both, will arrive in only a minute.

"What are you going to do?" I say. "You don't have any leverage here. The cops are coming, and this isn't going to end well for you."

It's not going to end well for me, either, but I don't have time to quibble over that little detail. As long as he's got a hostage, I'm not going anywhere.

Poppa Bear turns his head slightly, toward the sound of the cops. It's a chance to take a shot, but I can't be sure I won't hit Cassidy. He's got her locked in tight, in front of his body. Maybe I can hit one of the burly man's love handles poking out over the side, but if I don't drop him with a kill shot, he can easily end her before I'll have a second chance.

He looks back at me. Panic etched on his face. He doesn't know what to do, and he's going to run out of time before he can commit. Which means I will also run out of time. The smart thing is for me to toss the pistol and get the hell out of here. Put as much distance between me and the cops as possible.

But I can't. I have to help Cassidy.

Poppa Bear's head swivels around a few more times, to me, to the road behind him, back again.

I can see his gritted teeth from here. The terror and indecision on his face.

But then, his expression changes. The tension wipes away. Lights of the police cars emerge through the trees to my left. They'll arrive in ten or fifteen seconds.

He pulls his gun arm back, tensing it.

My heart stops. "Don't!"

I try to sprint forward, but it's too late. He shoves the barrel of his pistol against Cassidy's temple and pulls the trigger. Her head jerks left as a spray of blood ejects from the right side of her scalp. Eyes are open. Her knees give way, and Poppa Bear lets her fall. Blood splatters turn his shirt into a red mess in an instant.

I lift my gun and take a shot. The blast punches a hole in his ample belly, making it ripple. He stumbles back. Heaves a breath.

Then he turns and runs into the forest.

Cassidy crumples into a heap on the side of the road. Blood leaking out, filling cracks in the asphalt. Her head has ruptured and her brains spread out all over the highway. She's dead. No mistaking it.

I tried. I tried to help her, and I failed. She's dead, and I could have saved her. I didn't save her.

Cassidy is dead, and it's my fault. I let him do it.

A cop car flies around the bend beyond the trees. Now visible.

Poppa Bear is fleeing, disappearing into the woods. Shot in the gut, he might not last long. Or, he might survive and escape without paying any price for the terrible thing he's done to this poor young woman, lying dead on the ground.

I have to make a choice because I don't have time to do both things. Get my shoebox, or get Poppa Bear.

CHAPTER THIRTY-SEVEN

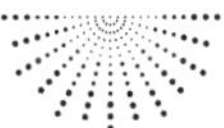

UTAH - FOUR YEARS AGO

Travis waved his pistol into the night air, indicating he wanted me to extricate myself from my rock prison. The light of the fire in the slot canyon made him look demonic. At his feet, the bound and gagged Pug could only watch as I rose, shrugging off the rocks that had brought me to the ground. Must have been a hundred of them.

I raised my hands in surrender, heart pounding so hard I couldn't hear the words Travis was speaking. He waved the gun toward the campfire, and I took a step. Knee ached. I wasn't sure which rock from Travis' homemade rock slide had done it, but there had been enough of them to do some damage. At least none of them had knocked me out and saddled me with a concussion.

"Over here," he said, waving the pistol toward the fire. I sat next to Pug, and Travis sat opposite us. Pistol out, over the fire. He seemed surprisingly calm. Maybe now that he had us both under his control and could kill us at any time, he had nothing else to worry about. Just a matter of pulling the trigger.

He paused, his eyes flicking over me. His face sported a strange expression. A little sad, maybe?

"You can take that tape off his face, if you want."

I reached over and mouthed *sorry* before I ripped the duct tape off Pug's lips. He winced.

"Your leg okay?" I said. Pug nodded.

I rubbed my knee a few times, willing the pain to go away. It had turned from a throb to an ache, and I checked it for anything broken inside. Gave my kneecap a few pushes in each direction, and it seemed to move okay. I'd never broken my knee before, so I wasn't sure what it was supposed to feel like.

"What happens now?" I asked, and then realized I didn't want to know the answer to that question.

"Now we talk," Travis said.

I nodded. This was good. If he had any reason to delay shooting us both in the head, that increased our chances. Between the two of us, Pug was the better conversationalist, so maybe he could engage in some verbal gymnastics. Reason with Travis. Then, I'd go for the gun when his attention slipped.

"First of all," Travis said, "I never stole from Gus. I never hurt his wife."

"Bullshit," Pug said.

The muscle-bound Asian shook his head. "It's easy for you to believe what you want. It's easy to just accept what they tell you is true, no matter what lies they're feeding you. Do you know what confirmation bias is?"

I shrugged, and Pug gave no response.

"Maybe you think you know what Gus does for a living?" Travis asked.

"What are you talking about?" I said.

"You ever hear the name Luis Velasquez?"

Pug and I shared a look. I hadn't, and I could tell from Pug's expression that he hadn't, either.

"What about Charlie? You guys remember him, right? Did you know he was my brother?"

I took in Travis' face, for the first time. I could see the family resemblance between Travis and Charlie. Charlie was a driver, just like me, but a few months ago he'd stopped coming around. When I asked about it, someone told me he'd moved to Chicago.

"I remember Charlie," Pug said. "What about him?"

"There was a story that he moved away."

"Right," I said.

"He didn't move. He's at the bottom of Grand Lake right now."

I leaned forward. "Why?"

"He was supposed to pick up Luis Velasquez from the airport one day. But, Charlie got into a small car accident on the way to the airport. No big deal; just a fender-bender. But, he knew he'd get in trouble if he was late, so he tried to leave. Turns out, there was a cop nearby who pulled him over for trying to flee the scene of an accident. That's a crime.

"So, Charlie goes to jail for a few hours, and Velasquez doesn't have a ride at the airport. When it's all sorted out, our mutual boss Gus knows Velasquez is upset, and he gets a call that Charlie was seen leaving a cop station with a bail bondsman. He didn't call anyone to come pick him up."

"So?" I said, but I knew where the story was headed. I could feel it, creeping into my bones.

"So, Gus assumed Charlie went to tell the cops that El Lobo was in town."

A chill ran up my spine. The name El Lobo was something whispered around the dorms at the Freedom House, or any gathering of our coworkers. Some kind of mythical creature, half man and half wolf. At least, that's what a few people made him out to be.

"You're saying this El Lobo is Luis Velasquez?" Pug said. His brow was creased on his tired face. But, if I wasn't mistaken, it appeared that Travis was beginning to get through to him, too.

But I still wasn't convinced. This could all be a story.

Travis nodded. "My brother is dead because of El Lobo. And I've been under suspicion ever since. I don't sleep at night. I keep guns all around my apartment, waiting for someone to slip inside in the middle of the night."

"What the hell are you talking about?" I said.

"I'll ask you again," Travis said. "What do you think Gus does for a living?"

"He runs bets," I said. "Mobile underground casinos and sports betting and stuff like that. That's what everyone says."

Slowly, menacingly, Travis shook his head. "Gus works for Velasquez. And Velasquez is a higher-up in the Sinaloa Cartel. Since we all work for Gus, that means *we* all work for the cartel, too."

"Bullshit," I said, but my resolve had waned to almost nothing. The conversations with Pug over the last couple days weighed on me. Pug's stories about the things we'd done. The things he'd seen. The conclusions were too hard to ignore.

I checked Pug's face, and his eyes had gone cold. Staring at the fire, I could see he believed Travis.

"Are you going to kill us now?" I asked. At that moment, I didn't think I would have the strength to wrestle the gun away from Travis. I could see Pug didn't, either.

Our captor shrugged. "I never wanted to kill you. All I wanted was for you to leave me alone. I thought if I came out here in the desert for a couple weeks, Gus would stop looking for me, eventually. But I was wrong about that, it seems."

For a few seconds, none of us said anything. We all stared at the fire as little embers floated into the sky.

"What happens next?" I said.

Travis sighed and then dug a hand into his backpack. He removed a headlamp which he slid over his head, resting on his brow.

"I'm going to leave you guys here. Walk out of this canyon and head back to my car. Then, I'm going to drive west. I'll ask that you not follow me. Maybe you can go back and tell Gus that you saw me and put a bullet in my head. I don't know if he'll believe that, but you can try. Or you can tell him you never found me, and then maybe he'll send someone else. Maybe this will never be over."

Travis stood and holstered his weapon, then he tossed Pug's gun on the ground, a few feet from us. "Are you going to follow me?"

Pug met my eyes, then he dipped his head. Pug didn't want to answer the question and was leaving it up to me. After all his fire over the last couple days, Pug was beaten. I could see it in his eyes.

"No," I said. "We'll leave you alone. But, answer me this: how did Gus know you would be out here?"

He shrugged. "I was wondering that myself, when I first spied you two stalking me. Then, I remembered. I made the mistake of once telling him how much I liked the Canyonlands. This district, specifically."

Travis turned to leave, but I held out my hand. "Wait. One more question."

He looped his thumbs inside his shoulder straps and nodded.

"Why did you run?" I said. "You stuck around at first after they killed your brother. What triggered this?"

"Gus or someone else sent a couple guys to my apartment last week to take me out. I guess they thought having the brother of a dead man around was too much trouble."

"And so that's it?" Pug said. "You'll just keep running?"

He shrugged. "For as long as I can. But I know I can't do it forever. If I've learned one thing over the last few years working for these people, it's that no one ever gets away from the Sinaloa."

CHAPTER THIRTY-EIGHT

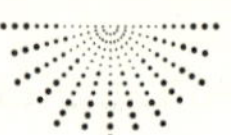

OKLAHOMA - NOW

I race around the other side of the RV and snatch the shoebox. The sirens echo off the far side of the vehicle, growing so loud they're filling my head. I can see the red and blue lights reflected off a nearby mile marker sign.

To my right, an open field. Barbed wire fencing, vast grass expanse stretching out forever. Going that way is suicide. The only thing left to do is hustle into the woods, in the same direction Poppa Bear fled. But, I should assume the cops saw him scurrying off that way and already have officers on foot after him.

If I go that way, I'll run into him, or the cops. Neither is something I want. But, it's also the only way remaining that will provide any cover. If I stay, I'm caught, with only a few seconds until it happens.

My eyes track along the open field, hoping to see a ditch, or a hill, or anything I can use for temporary shelter. But, there's nothing except an endless length of flat earth. Typical Oklahoma.

I don't have a choice. No way can I let them take me here. I've shot two people and wrecked an RV to kill a third. Even if I can prove I did all this in self-defense, I'm hosed when Gavin Belmont learns about it all. If he finds out about my shoebox, I'll probably go right back to jail. For good this time.

I wipe the gun with my t-shirt and toss it on top of the RV. If I am arrested, better chance of not being shot on sight if I'm unarmed. Not that I'm planning to be arrested, but I've been caught off guard in that respect before.

I bend my knees and draw one foot back, ready to sprint. I set my sights on a particular cluster of trees. There's a small stretch of open highway and then grass between here and there. Maybe fifty feet. Hidden by the RV, I can't see the cops from here. But I have a good idea of how close they are. I'll be exposed for one full second, maybe two.

Time to do this.

So I go. As fast as my legs will carry me, I'm racing toward the trees. When I emerge from the dark side of the RV, I can't tell if the cops are yelling at me. Can't tell if they're talking to me over the loudspeaker. All I hear is the wind whistling in my ears as my feet trod asphalt, and then grass, and then the broken twigs and brush. Shoebox whipping against the wind, clutched in my armpit. I'm never letting this thing go, ever again.

I run like this for thirty more seconds, deep into the forest, until I think my heart will explode. Have to stop. When I do, I look around and see no cops, no canine officers, no nothing. I can hear a loudspeaker back by the road, warning anyone in the RV to step out. The sound is far away, dim and echoing between the trees.

I squint and can make out an ambulance, with several uniforms rushing toward the downed bodies of Cassidy and Dichali. A pair of EMTs hauling a stretcher toward the RV. All they'll find inside is a dead Ash, loose bills, and a whole slew of drugs and weapons.

But it looks like they don't see me. I made it. I'm free.

For some reason, my knees go weak. I collapse to the ground. Chest heaving. Adrenaline dissipating, I'm overcome by the injuries piled up over the last few days. Hard to believe that, just a couple days ago, I dove out of the second-floor window of my old apartment. Still feel guilty about that, but it's not the worst thing I've done on the trip.

I feel anguish for Cassidy. She didn't deserve to die. Didn't deserve to be stuck with these people, doomed to be used as a pawn by the evil shithead Barry, AKA Poppa Bear. Also, I even feel a little heartache for Dichali. I didn't get to know him over the last few days, but he didn't seem like a terrible person. He even laughed at a few of my jokes. He was more like a guy with a personality too small to overcome Ash's menace.

When I look up, I note the sound of rushing water. I'm near a creek. I can see the steep decline of the earth toward the bank close to me, and the lush greenery nearby. Birds chirping. On a leaf next to my knee, a little red ladybug plods along, not a care in the world. I think I might still have some of that LSD coursing through my system. The colors are extra vibrant, or, at least, I think they are. I've never had anything else to compare it to.

I'm on a ridge, with the creek about twenty feet lower in elevation. If I have to hide, slinking down to that water will provide some cover for me. Good to know.

And then, I hear labored breathing. I turn my head to the right and see Poppa Bear, hiding behind a tree. A hundred feet away. His back is to me, and he's pushing up against it, resting. His shoulders heave up and down as he grunts. Bushy hair a mess, slicked with sweat and matted to his neck. His shirt is torn and dirty.

I can't see the blood spot on his belly from where I shot him, but I imagine it's still oozing blood. I've heard stories about people taking multiple bullets and surviving, of not even falling to the ground when shot. Seems Poppa Bear has a stronger constitution than I anticipated.

His gun is out, pointed back toward the RV. Why isn't he running away?

He must be plotting a way to return and recover his stash. That's insane. But, this man did kill his wife in cold blood only two minutes ago. Clearly, he's not in a lucid state of mind.

Now is my chance to sneak up on him. Of course, it would be better for me to turn in the other direction and get the hell out of here, but I can't do that.

For what he's done, he has to pay.

I slip the knife from my pocket and extend the blade. Set the shoebox down next to me, and then I creep toward him. I hate killing people. Hate involving myself in deaths that could have been prevented. But, if someone deserves to die, it's this man. He killed Cassidy without giving it any thought because she was no longer useful to him.

I raise the knife. Come within a few feet of his hulking frame.

I lunge and drive the knife into the center of his back. He emits a horrible bellow and shoots straight up, one hand immediately trying to reach behind him to dislodge the blade.

Before he can, I yank it free. I'm preparing to plunge it into him again when I hear the sound of sticks and leaves shuffling. Oncoming footsteps. Gathering, speeding up, closing in on our location.

Cops. Has to be cops.

I bolt, snatching the shoebox along the way. He's staggering, still trying to reach to his back and claw at the wound there, now ballooning into a red wedge on his shirt.

I head toward the steep ridge next to the river bank. Just before I descend to the river, I look back as Poppa Bear sinks to his knees. And I see two officers closing in on him, weapons drawn.

CHAPTER THIRTY-NINE

OKLAHOMA - NOW

I move along the curve of the river, keeping my head down. Shielded by the high banks on either side, as long as I stay on this path, I can get away. I have a chance to get away.

With a foggy brain, I'm navigating away from the scene of the RV crash, back toward the road up ahead. I have the shoebox. I have money now. Cassidy said there's a bus station in Guymon, so I have the means to return to Denver.

After about thirty seconds, I hear two quick blasts of a gun. A person moaning.

He's gone. Poppa Bear refused to surrender, and the cops have killed him. But, now they're going to want to find the person who shot and stabbed him. I can't let them do that.

I press on, adding a little hustle to my steps. The faster

I can get out of here, the less I have to worry about these cops, who must be close on my heels. It's reasonable to assume they might have seen me sprinting away from the RV, so they'll have people out looking for me. Dogs, too, if I'm unlucky.

I hear that moan again, from back where the cops closed in on Poppa Bear. But, the moan is all wrong. It doesn't sound like Poppa Bear. It's not his deep and throaty timbre. Then, I realize two separate voices are moaning, not a single one.

Did he shoot the cops?

I need to run. Get the hell out of here. If he's not dead, I'm still in jeopardy. But how could he not be dead?

I don't have to puzzle over that for long. Two seconds later, his bulky head appears at the top of the river bank. Gun extended out toward me.

"Hi, Micah."

The front of his shirt is stained burgundy from where I shot him in the belly. With all that girth, I'm not surprised it didn't send him to the ground. I should have shot him in the head. Not only that, I should have done it *yesterday*. If I'd killed him the day before, Cassidy would still be alive right now. Those cops he probably killed would still be alive.

He flicks the gun toward him, inviting me to ascend the bank to rise to his level.

"Did you shoot those two cops? Are they dead back there?"

He sighs. "Tell me what's in your shoebox. I've been dying to know. I didn't think it was a big deal before, you know, because every man is allowed to have his secrets. But it's gotta be something major for you to go to all this trouble. My wife and two of my best friends are dead because you walked into my life. That's not nothing, brother, and I think I deserve some answers."

"You deserve to eat a bullet, you piece of shit. Their deaths are not on me. You came up to *me* at Eskimo Joe's. You started all this. And *you* killed your wife, asshole. Don't blame this on me like it's some pre-destined thing that happened because I was at the bar two days ago."

He swishes his lips around and then grimaces. His big frame leans forward, anguish on his hairy face. Those injuries have to be weighing on him.

Then, he flicks the gun toward him again. "I don't have time to bargain with you, Micah. Come up here with me now, or I shoot you where you stand."

Not much of a choice. I climb up the bank, now on an even level with him. Steal a quick look over his shoulder for more cops. There have to be more than the two nearby. But, I'm honestly not sure if it's better for them to show up right now or not. Not sure which one of us they would shoot. Probably both, just to be safe.

"What's in the shoebox?"

"None of your business."

He eyes it, a look of childish anticipation on his face. "Bring it over to me. I want to see for myself."

"I don't think so."

"Do it, or I put four slugs in your stomach and leave you here to die." When I pause and glance past him again, he grins. "There are no more pigs here right now. Everyone else back there is emergency personnel. Going to be another five or ten minutes before more police show up to save your lying ass. So, pretty please, come over here and let me see what's in your magic box of secrets."

"Why should I?"

"Show me what's in it, and I'll let you walk away. Don't, and I'll kill you, and then I'll find out what's in it, anyway."

With gritted teeth, I march across the bank of the river, holding the shoebox out in front. With each step, the excitement on his face grows. Maybe he suspects he'll bleed out, so he wants this last question answered before he dies. That red spot on his stomach grows larger by the second.

When I reach within about four feet, he holds out a hand. Shakes his head.

"Whoa, stay there. That's close enough. It's not like we're going to hug it out or anything. You jump or try to run, you eat a bullet. Get it?"

"I got it."

"Now, open it up and let me see your buried treasure."

I reach one hand up and take off the lid. As he leans over to close the gap between us, I hurl the shoebox up into the air. The contents come flying out, spreading like a flock of birds. Photos, bits of paper, plastic flash drives, all hurtle into the sky above us. Glimpses of white and red and black and blue and green blur into the air.

His neck cranes as his eyes instinctively travel up to follow the items. With my right hand, I make a fist and swing at his face. My left hand reaches out to snatch his gun.

I connect with my right fist, smashing it against his nose. Feel it crumple against his jawbone. A mountain of hair flattens against my knuckles when they dive through his beard.

My left hand closes around the top of the barrel of the pistol, and I yank back. It easily comes free from his grasp. I snatch it away, back toward my body. Out of reach. His eyes are closed, his face smushed from my punch.

I pop him again in the mouth with another quick right, and he staggers. As pictures and pieces of paper float through the air around me, settling into the mushy foliage, I reach into my pocket and draw the blade. I have to drop his gun to flick it open. A *snick* fills my ears as the knife extends, ready to go to work. Then I shove it forward.

The tip pierces his neck. I push until my hand brushes against the protruding beard. Until I can feel the wetness of his blood against my hand. His eyes are wide, his mouth open. He tries to heave in a breath, but he looks so startled, it doesn't seem like he can. Big chest hiccuping. His face vibrates, jittering left and right.

He staggers back and slaps frenzied hands at the blade jutting from him. He manages to pull the knife out of his neck, causing a torrent to flow. Blood covering his hands like red gloves. One step back, his eyes wide, gasping for air. Red pours out of the hole faster and faster, like a neck-tie. Then, another step to the edge of the rim of the creek.

He falls backward, sliding down the small hill. I listen to his body somersault the last twenty feet to the lip of the water.

Frantic, I wipe the knife blade on the grass and then clean my fingerprints off the hilt. Holding it by my shirt, I fling it down onto the bank of the creek with him. I do the same with his gun, although I'm not sure it will have my fingerprints on it.

More cops have to be incoming soon, despite what he said. I need to get out of here now. Get to Guymon, buy a bus ticket, and return to Denver. It's not too late. I can still do this.

Before I leave, I take one look down to the creek. Poppa Bear is sprawled next to the rushing water, his eyes open. Not moving. The front of his shirt is one solid block of red.

Now, I collect the items from my shoebox and scramble away, toward the woods, to my freedom.

CHAPTER FORTY

COLORADO - NOW

When I open my eyes, the first thing I notice is Mile High Stadium, from the window of my seat on the bus. I smile, but not from joy. It's relief. Weary, broken, unsettled relief.

Denver is not my home. It hasn't felt like that for the few months I've lived here. I don't have any prospects or anything to provide hope for the future.

But I'm alive, and I have the shoebox. I do have a past, even though it's a secret no one else can ever know. And that secret is sitting on the empty seat next to me. After everything I went through to get this thing back, I'm never letting it out of my sight again. Michael McBriar no longer exists, but as long as I have this shoebox, a part of him will live on through me.

I check my phone. It's eight o'clock on Friday morning. Gavin Belmont had said he'd be here by late morning for brunch, but that doesn't tell me much of anything. I note he hasn't called me yet today, so I can reasonably assume he's not in town yet. Maybe still on his plane.

I just might make it home unscathed.

My thoughts drift to a few months ago, as Gavin introduced me to the condo in lower downtown Denver. The one the government bought for me as part of my deal to testify against Luis Velasquez and other key members of the Sinaloa cartel. Being in the apartment made me feel guilty. It would be the largest place I'd lived in since my parents' house, by a significant amount. Felt opulent, like I didn't deserve it. Gavin felt that way too, apparently, because he sneered at me the whole time as he gave me the tour. "If I could install cameras here to make sure you're behaving," he said, "I would."

He's been antagonistic to me since the beginning. Since our first meeting when I was in prison in Ohio. He replaced a case worker I actually got along with. A fed I didn't think was a terrible person. And I knew right away that Gavin wasn't happy about his assignment, either. Our relationship has only become more strained over these months.

But I don't want to think about him anymore, even though I have to see him today. Just give me another hour or two of peace. Time to shake this icky feeling off me.

I don't want to think about everything that has happened over the last four days. Don't want to think about Cassidy, the woman who seduced me and then died at the hands of her jealous husband, right before my eyes. I don't want to consider the role I played in her death.

It's too heavy to ponder. I've had way too much death in my life over the last couple years. When do I reach the place where I can relax and not worry about chaos saturating my waking hours?

I do keep rehashing that crazy dream I had about my friend coming to visit me in the woods. But, I'm not sure if it was actually a dream, or maybe a hallucination. Either way, it doesn't matter. All I have left of the best friend I ever knew now sits in this shoebox on the bus with me. As soon as I get home, it's going in the floorboards in my bedroom, and never coming out again. It will stay there, so I know it's safe.

In another twenty minutes, the bus pulls into Union Station, which is convenient, since I live essentially across the street. I plan to grab a shower and then show up at Frank's office, ready to work. Not sure how I'm going to get there, since my butchered Camry is somewhere back in Oklahoma, probably sitting in an impound lot.

Maybe I'll go car shopping later today. Get a Honda this time. I've had my eye on a used Accord on Craigslist for a couple weeks now, surprised each time I check that it's still there. Or maybe taking a lunch at work today is a bad idea. I'm not sure if Frank will yell at me for disappearing for several days without checking in. Somehow, I don't think he will. Frank seems like a good guy. A reasonable old man.

The bus comes to a stop underneath Union Station, so I grab my shoebox and stretch my legs as I stand. All night long on a bus is exhausting.

I shuffle through the line ahead of me, waiting to disembark, and when I near the front of the line, I keep my head down and use the guardrail to descend. Feet clomp down the steps, and the dry, Colorado air sucks the moisture from my skin as soon as I encounter it.

I'm off the bus. And when I look up, I see US Marshal Gavin Belmont, standing there on the sidewalk.

His arms crossed, his sunglasses on. Sneering at me.

"Come with me," he says.

He pivots and walks away from the people streaming out of the buses, toward an empty spot near the doors leading into the concourse. I plod over to him, stepping onto the sidewalk next to the area where the buses park.

He snatches me by the arm and pulls me close. "Bet you think you're clever," he says, just loud enough for me to hear.

"Apparently not," I say. I'm trying to sound tough, but I don't feel it. I feel like a kid who got caught playing with matches. The shoebox is clutched under one arm, near my waist, a little behind me. If he asks what's in the box, then this is all over.

"What happened to your face?"

Instinctively, my finger touches my cheek. There are a dozen little scabs there, from the bits of broken glass when the RV wrecked.

"It's nothing. A mirror broke."

"Hmm. I'll bet. Do you have any idea of the potential damage you could have caused? How much cleanup I've had to do to cover your tracks?" When I say nothing, he continues. "What were you doing in Oklahoma? Going to see an old girlfriend? Feeling nostalgic about your old college life and wanted to hit up a few bars?"

Interesting. So, he knows about Stillwater, likely because of my impounded car. Was only a matter of time before that info made its way around. And, he knows about this bus ride home. But, there's a good chance he doesn't know about anything in between.

I have to hope he knows nothing else.

"Something like that," I say.

"Well, I hope it was worth it. Because you're in a shit-load of trouble, you little miscreant."

"No."

His head jerks a fraction of an inch. "Excuse me?"

"I don't think so, Gavin. I want out."

"What are you saying?"

"I want out of the program. I want to be on my own, so I don't have to be your problem anymore. So I can be free."

He grins. "You have no idea the consequences of what you're saying."

"Maybe not, but I have to be my own man. I have to stand on my own. If I'm not in WitSec any longer, then you won't have to worry about me and waste resources keeping me in check. It's win-win, as far as I can see."

He leans back against the wall and folds his arms across his chest. "You're making a massive mistake."

"Maybe so, but it's my mistake to make."

"Fine. I'll need it in writing."

"Sure, whatever."

He leans in close to me. "Your old buddies from the Sinaloa cartel? They're going to catch up to you. They're going to find you and drop you into a stack of tires so they can douse you with gasoline and watch you burn. And when they do, there's not a thing I can do to help you. Do you understand? That's the decision you're rushing to make here."

I stand, stone-faced. Say nothing.

He shakes his head and gives a little laugh of incredulity. "Okay, Micah Reed. if you put even one civilian life in danger, I'll break both of your legs. Also, it's been nice knowing you. You're on your own now."

With that, he struts away from me, out into the open air.

I'm on my own now.

No one watching over me, checking up on me, protecting me, judging me.

I'm free.

READY FOR THE SEQUEL?

To find out when the next book is coming, join the Reader Group at www.jimheskett.com

AFTERWORD

A NOTE TO READERS

Want to know when the next book is coming out? Join my mailing list to get updates and free stuff!

If you started reading Micah Reed's adventure with this book, go back and take a peek at Airbag Scars. Micah's backstory will make a lot more sense, and you can get this full length novel FOR FREE at www.jimheskett.com

With that out of the way, thank you for reading my book!

The flashback story in Utah was originally supposed to be its own novel, but when I realized how it needed to end (quietly, with no big action sequence), I think it works better this way. The two stories—two sides of Micah—

balance each other and provide some suspense as we jump back and forth. But, this story did have a little more real-life inspiration than usual… see the next page for a crazy story that became part of the basis of this book.

Please consider leaving reviews on Amazon and Goodreads. I know it's a pain, but you have no idea how much it will help the success of this book and my ability to write future books. That, sharing it on social media, and telling other people to read it.

Are you interested in joining a Facebook community of Jim Heskett fiction fans? Discuss the books with other people, including the author! Join for free at www.jimheskett.com/bookophile

I have a website where you can learn more about me and my other projects. Check me out at www.jimheskett.com and sign up for my reader group so you can stay informed on the latest news. You'll even get some freebies for signing up. You like free stuff, right?

THE CAR CHASE

While I no longer drink or do drugs, when I was young, I was quite wild. Since this book deals with some heavy drug use, I thought it might a good time to tell a story. Here is the tale of how I was once in a car chase while tripping on LSD. Seriously.

Danny and I ate acid one sunny spring day in Tulsa. It was his first time, and we had no grand plans other than to just drive around in my red Ford Bronco and experience life. We drove to some parking lot and pretended it was Disney World. We went to a park and played on the big toy. We pretended that the sand was water full of sharks and you couldn't touch the ground or you'd die.

Later, we were driving through Woodward Park, and Danny was playing with an empty BubbleTape container. I don't even know if they sell this brand of gum anymore, but it's plastic, about the size of a can of tobacco.

The LSD was worming through Danny's system, and he was chewing piece after piece of gum. Then, he finished the last piece, and he rolled down his window and threw the empty container at some random car. I was a little shocked, a little not sure if this was really happening.

To our surprise, the car was full of rednecks, and their car started up. Headlights came on. My heart raced, thumping against the inside of my ribcage. Danny had thrown something at a car!

They took off after us, though the park. They chased us to 21st and Utica, and I stopped at the red light. Danny was screaming "GO! GO!" But I said, "I can't, it's a red light."

One of Danny's victims got out of his car, two or three behind us, and stalked up toward my car. I watched him in the side mirror. Fists balled. He started banging on Danny's window. Hard enough to make the window bend.

Danny's screaming. Telling us, we have to escape, now. I locked the door and then when the light was green I took off.

I turned right into the pretty neighborhoods around an expensive private school. They chased us. Danny cheered me on while I made lefts and rights trying to lose them. He said something like, "I bet they run out of gas before us."

Turn after turn, I kept winding through the neighborhood, my heart in my throat. They wouldn't give up the pursuit.

Finally, I had to pull a move. Knew we couldn't keep this up forever. I hit the gas down a street and took a hard left, and then another hard right onto the nearest side street. Suddenly, I couldn't see them in my rearview anymore, and then when we were safely a few blocks away, we shouted and cheered. At that moment we were movie stars in a great car chase.

Side note: don't do drugs, but especially, don't drive when you're on drugs. Just because I was wild in my youth and made it to the other side alive doesn't mean you will, too.

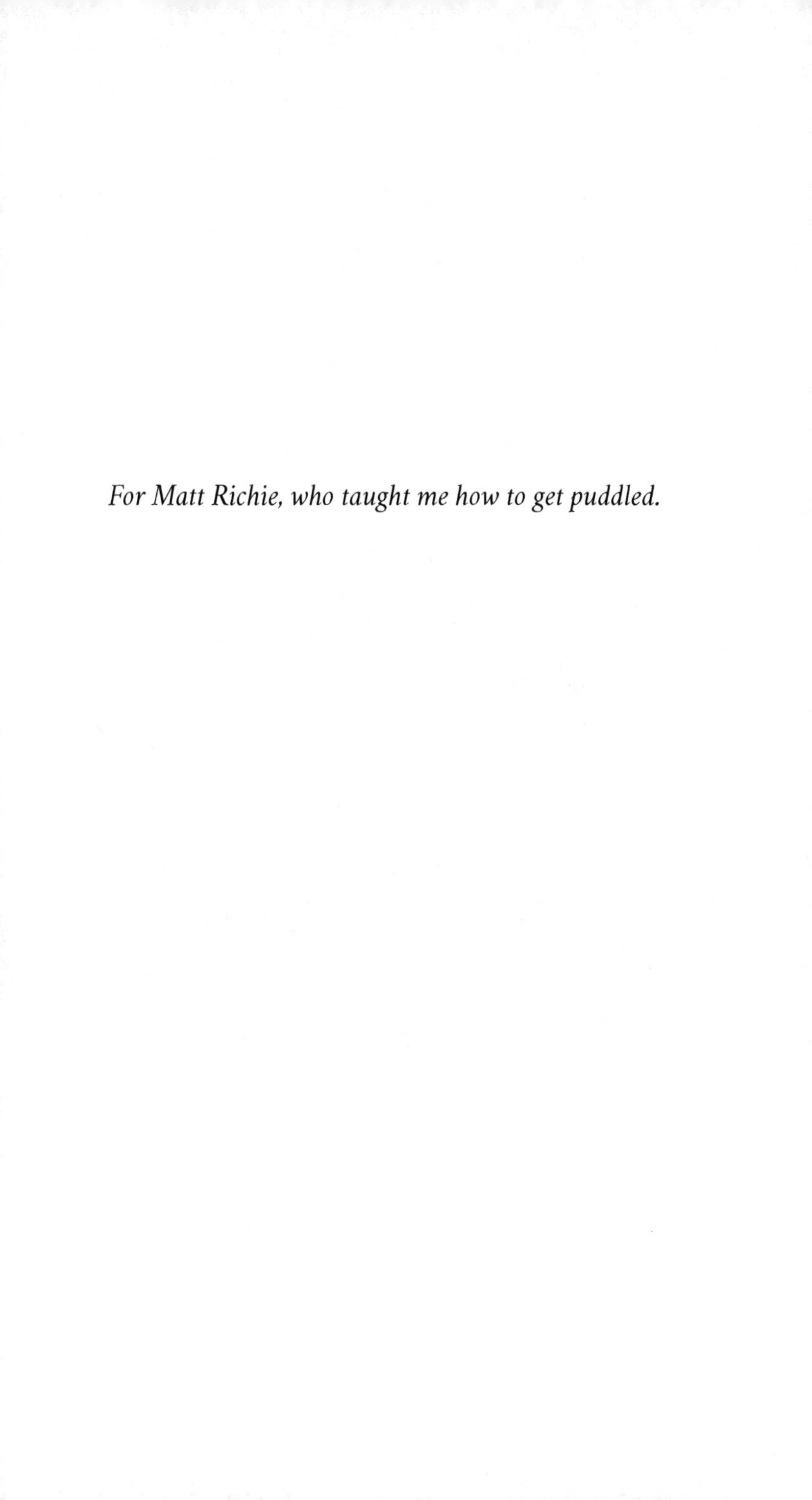

For Matt Richie, who taught me how to get puddled.

Published by Royal Arch Books

Www.RoyalArchBooks.com

Please consider leaving a review once you have finished this book. Want to know when the next book is coming out?
Join my mailing list to get updates and free stuff!

TIMELINE

Micah Reed Chronology:

While the Micah Reed novels are essentially standalone stories, each one does build on some elements from previous books. To see the list of how each story fits on the overall timeline, visit www.jimheskett.com/chron. If you want to read them in order, check out that link.

BOOKS BY JIM HESKETT

For a full list of all Jim Heskett's books, please visit www.RoyalArchBooks.com

If you like thrillers, you'll want to take a gander at my Whistleblower Trilogy. The first book, Wounded Animals, follows the story of Tucker Candle, who meets a mysterious stranger who warns him not to take a business trip. Candle goes, however, and when he comes home, he discovers a dead man in his bathroom and his wife is missing.

ABOUT THE AUTHOR

Jim Heskett was born in the wilds of Oklahoma, raised by a pack of wolves with a station wagon and a membership card to the local public swimming pool. Just like the man in the John Denver song, he moved to Colorado in the summer of his 27th year, and never looked back. Aside from an extended break traveling the world, he hasn't let the Flatirons mountains out of his sight.

He fell in love with writing at the age of fourteen with a copy of Stephen King's The Shining. Poetry became his first outlet for teen angst, then later some terrible screenplays, and eventually short and long fiction. In between, he worked a few careers that never quite tickled his creative toes, and hasn't ever forgotten about Stephen King. You can find him currently huddled over a laptop in an undisclosed location in Colorado, dreaming up ways to kill beloved characters.

You can also scour the internet to find the occasional guest post or podcast appearance. A curated list of media appearances can be found at www.jimheskett.com/media.

He believes the huckleberry is the king of berries and refuses to be persuaded in any other direction.

If you'd like to ask a question or just to say hi, stop by www.jimheskett.com/about and fill out the contact form.

www.jimheskett.com

Made in the USA
San Bernardino, CA
11 May 2019